## "Go back to sleep,"

Joe said, conscious of the sudden thickness in his voice.

Sara bit her lower lip and shook her head. "Too scared. What a wimp, huh?"

"I'm here."

"You weren't *here*. You were *there*." She pointed in the direction of the den. "God. I don't think I'll ever sleep again."

He didn't like where this was heading. Not one bit. Because he knew when she turned those big green eyes up at him and asked him to stay with her, here in her room, he'd say the dumbest, most dangerous thing he'd ever said. *Yes*.

Dear Reader,

What is there to say about a month with a new Nora Roberts title except "Hurry up and get to the store!" *Enchanted* is a mysterious, romantic and utterly irresistible follow-up to THE DONOVAN LEGACY trilogy, which appeared several years ago and is currently being reissued. It's the kind of story only Nora can tell—and boy, will you be glad she did!

The rest of our month is pretty special, too, so pick up a few more books to keep you warm. Try *The Admiral's Bride,* by Suzanne Brockmann, the latest TALL, DARK & DANGEROUS title. These navy SEAL heroes are fast staking claim to readers' hearts all over the world. Read about the last of THE SISTERS WASKOWITZ in Kathleen Creighton's *Eve's Wedding Knight.* You'll love it—and you'll join me in hoping we revisit these fascinating women—and their irresistible heroes—someday. *Rio Grande Wedding* is the latest from multiaward-winning Ruth Wind, a part of her MEN OF THE LAND miniseries, featuring the kind of Southwestern men no self-respecting heroine can resist. Take a look at Vickie Taylor's *Virgin Without a Memory,* a book *you'll* remember for a long time. And finally, welcome Harlequin Historical author Mary McBride to the contemporary romance lineup. *Just One Look* will demand more than just one look from you, and it will have you counting the days until she sets another story in the present day.

And, of course, mark your calendar and come back next month, when Silhouette Intimate Moments will once again bring you six of the most excitingly romantic novels you'll ever find.

Enjoy!

*Leslie J. Wainger*

Leslie J. Wainger
Executive Senior Editor

Please address questions and book requests to:
Silhouette Reader Service
U.S.: 3010 Walden Ave., P.O. Box 1325, Buffalo, NY 14269
Canadian: P.O. Box 609, Fort Erie, Ont. L2A 5X3

# JUST ONE LOOK

## MARY McBRIDE

*Silhouette*®
INTIMATE™ MOMENTS®

Published by Silhouette Books

**America's Publisher of Contemporary Romance**

**SILHOUETTE BOOKS**

ISBN 0-373-07966-4

JUST ONE LOOK

Copyright © 1999 by Mary Myers

**Books by Mary McBride**

Silhouette Intimate Moments

*Just One Look* #966

Harlequin Historicals

*Riverbend* #164
*Fly Away Home* #189
*The Fourth of Forever* #221
*The Sugarman* #237
*The Gunslinger* #256
*Forever and a Day* #294
*Darling Jack* #323
*Quicksilver's Catch* #375
*Storming Paradise* #424
*The Marriage Knot* #465

Harlequin Books

*Outlaw Brides*
"The Ballad of Josie Dove"

---

## MARY McBRIDE

When it comes to writing romance, Mary McBride is a natural. What else would anyone expect from someone whose parents met on a blind date on Valentine's Day, and who met her own husband—whose middle name just happens to be Valentine—on February 14, as well?

Although *Just One Look* is Mary's first contemporary romance, she is no stranger to publishing. She has written ten historical romances for Harlequin Historicals, most recently *The Marriage Knot,* a June 1999 release.

She lives in St. Louis, Missouri, with her husband and two sons. Mary loves to hear from readers. You can write to her c/o P.O. Box 411202, St. Louis, MO 63141.

For Barbara M. Falk
Thanks for the coffee, comfort and care.

# Chapter 1

Sara Campbell never saw it coming.

She was stuck in traffic three blocks from home, and once she got there she wasn't going to leave again. Never. Ever. From now on, she was going to say no to therapy that didn't help panic attacks, tranquilizers that never calmed her down, and all the dopey coping strategies that didn't work.

She was going home and she was going to stay there. Period.

"You're making a huge mistake," Dr. Bourne had said just twenty minutes ago in his overheated, over-decorated office when Sara had told him this would be her final session. "Please reconsider, Sara."

"No, I won't. Can't you see the logic of it, Dr. Bourne? My problem is panic attacks, right? But I only have the attacks when I leave home. So, if I don't leave home anymore, I'm cured."

Sara had added a tiny little *ta-da* to her declaration

of independence, which hadn't amused Dr. Bourne one bit. In fact, it had made the psychiatrist sit forward in his flame-stitched wing chair and positively glower over his tortoiseshell reading glasses.

"This is serious," he said.

"I know. I'm very serious."

"You're a young woman, Sara. You're what…?" He glanced down at her file. "Thirty-one years old. Not only young, but attractive, too. You can't just close the door on the world."

"Oh, no?" She grabbed her purse and stood. "Watch me."

Now she was just three blocks from home. In a minute or two, once the stalled traffic started up again, the big tires of her Land Cruiser, her fortress on wheels, would be sounding that familiar, homecoming crunch on the gravel drive. She was going to press the remote almost sensuously to open the garage door, then drive in slowly, turn off the ignition, pull out the key and close the door behind her. For good.

The doctor was wrong. She wasn't going to be a prisoner in her own house. She was going to be free.

A raindrop splashed on the windshield, then another and another. Sara switched the wipers on and nudged up the heat against the November cold. It was perfect weather for a recluse, she thought. She'd build a fire in the den tonight, maybe put on her long and slinky black velour lounger, then fix herself a gooey grilled cheese sandwich and open a bottle of Merlot.

She'd go to sleep peacefully tonight knowing there was nowhere she had to go tomorrow. Or the next day. Or the next. No more making up dumb excuses. No more last-minute cancellations when she couldn't come up with a dumb excuse. No more worrying, stewing, fretting, sweating. Just no. No. No. No.

The world would have to come to her from now on. And the beauty of it was that it could, compliments of IBM, AT&T, UPS and 1-800-Everything.

The car behind her honked, making Sara realize she'd been sitting there for quite a while. She turned the wipers up a notch against the rain and peered at the two cars in front of her. Apparently the first one in line had stalled. Its driver, a huge man in a buffalo plaid jacket, was just getting out to glare at the motionless vehicle. After his glare accomplished nothing, he kicked the front tire and then walked around to open the hood.

The car behind her honked again, this time a bit more aggressively. Her windows were beginning to fog up, but when Sara glanced in the rearview mirror she was able to see a rude middle finger stabbing in her direction. ''Oh, great,'' she muttered, sorely tempted just then to return the gesture as a kind of final salute to the world and all the honkers and bird flippers in it.

She was too close to the car in front of her to maneuver around it. And even if she could, at almost rush hour, the oncoming traffic was already horrific, whizzing past on her left with barely a break in it. She was three blocks from home—home!—sanctuary!—and she was trapped.

Then, to make matters worse, the rain changed to sleet, and instead of splashing gently on her windshield, it started hitting hard and accumulating on the wipers so that every pass across the glass only made it more difficult to see. Behind her, the idiot attached to the finger honked again. And again. *Beep.*

Then it started. Sara's heart picked up speed. Her

grip on the steering wheel got slippery. Her vision blurred at the edges. Her breath came in short little gasps as the dark shroud of panic descended on her, threatening to smother her.

"Oh, please, no. Not now. Not here." She closed her eyes and clenched her teeth against the onslaught of the adrenaline rushing through her, her body's dire signal of danger, what the shrinks called "fight or flight." But she didn't know how to fight it. Trapped like this, she couldn't flee. It wasn't fair. Not now. She was almost home. Almost safe. Almost free.

*Beep.*

She forced her eyes open and squinted through the slush on the windshield to see the man in the buffalo plaid jacket—a blur of red and black—drop the hood on his car and get in. A second later a plume of greasy smoke rose from his exhaust and the stalled car appeared to shiver slightly, then shimmy to life. The light turned green, and he chugged across the intersection.

"Oh, thank God." Sara tightened her clammy grasp on the wheel and pressed her foot on the Land Cruiser's accelerator. The engine roared, but the Cruiser didn't move.

"What the...?"

Her heart pumped even harder. What? Had her engine frozen? Was she out of gas? Was the Cruiser flooded or dead? What was wrong?

She'd always meant to learn where the button for the hazard lights was located and how to lift the hood and change a tire and pump her own gas, but she hadn't learned and she hadn't put a blanket in the back or a shovel or granola bars or any of that winter emergency stuff. And this was definitely an emergency, since she hadn't bothered to wear her heavy winter coat or her gloves or a hat. God! She didn't even have panty hose on, let alone thick warm socks. Her fortress on wheels had suddenly become a chamber of horrors, and she was—

"Oh."

She looked down and realized that she had put the car in parking gear when it seemed as if she'd be stuck there for a while. Quickly, she shifted into forward gear, stepped on the gas again, then—after going a mere ten or fifteen feet—slammed on the brakes when the amber caution light changed to a hideous red.

*Beep!*

She was only three blocks away, but she was never going to get home. There would be no ceremonial closing of the garage door. She wouldn't be lighting a fire in the fireplace, or changing into her soft velour lounger, or reading in a comfy corner of her couch while she sipped a rich, full-bodied Merlot. She was going to be here forever—stopped at a permanent red light at this gray, slippery intersection with her palms dripping sweat and her head throbbing and her heart about to explode and some jerk behind her giving her the finger while he wasn't laying on the horn.

She was going to *die!*

The light changed to green.

Maybe she'd live after all. She could breathe, and drew in a long, deep breath just to prove it. Her head stopped throbbing and her heart felt more like a heart, not a bomb about to go off. Three blocks. Three minutes more. Four at the most. Then she'd be home for good. She'd be safe forever.

She stepped on the gas. The back tires spun a second on the sleet-covered street, then grabbed.

She was halfway across the intersection, but Sara

never saw the pickup truck until it slammed into her left front fender.

Joe Decker pumped the brakes, but the big unmarked Crown Victoria started to fishtail on the slick street in spite of his efforts and then nearly jumped the curb before he wrestled it to a halt.

Beside him, his partner's face went an even paler shade of white than it had been during their pursuit of the pickup. Sergeant Maggie O'Connor had braced for a crash, and when it hadn't happened, she blistered him with one of her Irish curses.

"Dammit, Decker! You suicidal son of a bitch. This guy isn't worth dying for. Do you hear me?"

He heard her but he didn't reply because he was already out of the car and racing through the snarl of stopped traffic toward the intersection where the pickup had smashed into the black Land Cruiser. The street was like a skating rink under his feet, and for somebody who could still do a pretty good imitation of a four-minute mile, Joe felt as if he was going in slippery slow motion. Sleet pelted his unshaven cheeks, and his breath seemed to freeze in front of him as soon as it escaped.

The closer he got to the intersection, the less space there was between vehicles. He vaulted over the hood of a Buick, then felt his feet going out from beneath him as he landed. He cursed all the way down to the cold, wet pavement, then cursed as he got back on his feet. The Buick's driver rolled down his window and added a few choice words of his own, but Joe wasn't listening because just up ahead he saw the hooded man exit the disabled pickup and lunge for the door of the Land Cruiser.

He reached under his jacket for his gun. "Stop. Police."

The perp had already jerked open the Cruiser's door and was trying to pull the female driver from her seat. Joe heard her shriek as he threaded the narrow spaces between cars, and all of a sudden he saw her reach up and rip the ski mask from her assailant's face.

"Turn around, you bastard," Joe screamed. "I want to see your face just once before I blow it away." He brought up his left hand to brace his right as he aimed his gun. *Don't move, lady,* he prayed.

But she did, dammit, and Joe had no choice but to lower his weapon and continue toward them. Where the hell was Maggie, anyway? He glanced quickly over his shoulder and saw that his partner was still in the car, calling for backup. He cursed roughly. By the time anybody got through this traffic, their man would be home, thumbing through the phone book for his next victim.

Joe had almost reached the snarled intersection when the unmasked man pulled back his gloved fist and let the scrappy little woman have it right in the side of her head. They both went down out of Joe's line of sight for a minute, and the next thing he saw was the perp—masked again—on the opposite side of the Land Cruiser and starting to run, slipping and sliding, east on Hartford toward Patriot's Park.

"That's it, asshole," Joe muttered. "I've got you now. I know every nook and cranny and culvert over there."

He was at the intersection, about to race around the Land Cruiser, when he saw the little redhead lying on the pavement. He stopped, absolutely still, while his heart bunched up in his chest and his breath chuffed out of his lungs.

Edie? No, it couldn't be. His wife had been dead for three years. For an instant, though, it was as if she was dying all over again, lying broken and bleeding on a winter street, sleet coming down and accumulating on her closed eyelids faster than he could wipe it away, and his tears freezing on her face and sirens—too late!—wailing in the cold distance.

Everything around him disappeared…except the woman lying at his feet. Joe shrugged out of his jacket and knelt to blanket her as best he could, all the while thinking, *Little idiot, didn't anybody tell you to bundle up on a day like this? Where's your plaid scarf with the fringe? Where's your silly hat with the floppy tassel? Why didn't you wear your gloves?*

Her hand was freezing as he clasped it in his own while he felt for a pulse. Yes! It was thready, but it was there. *I won't let you die. Not again.*

"Decker? She okay?"

"Call an ambulance, Maggie."

"It's already on the way. Did you get a look at our guy?"

Joe shook his head. "No." He used his thumb to gently wipe the sleet from the woman's pale eyelids. "But she did."

# *Chapter 2*

It was a sad fact of Lieutenant Joe Decker's life that the emergency room of Saint Catherine's was just about his second home. His name was even on the ante-up-for-coffee list in the staff lounge. He folded a dollar bill and shoved it through the slot in the top of the jar before he poured the last inch of black sludge from the pot.

"Where do you buy this stuff? Wanda's Bait and Party Shop?" he grumbled after his first sip.

"How'd you guess?" Lucy Mack was taking a break from her stint on triage, and she laughed out loud, a sound not heard all that often in this particular corner of Saint Cat's, especially on an icy November night when business was brisk with fender benders and broken bones. She was a pretty blonde with soft blue eyes, an intriguing dimple in her chin and world-class ankles beneath her white stockings. Joe had thought more than once about asking her out sometime, but the thought had never quite progressed from his brain to his lips.

"How's the shoulder, Decker?" She grinned. "Met up with any more steel doors lately?"

Just three weeks earlier he'd separated his shoulder during a drug bust when the Alcohol, Tobacco and Firearms idiots forgot the battering ram and he'd underestimated the door in question. He'd gotten the sucker open, though, even if it had nearly torn him in half. "Good thing I didn't use my head, huh?"

"I don't know. Maybe you should have." Lucy laughed again, then her pretty face darkened in a frown. "That woman you brought in," she said. "Did I hear somebody say that she actually saw the South Side Ripper?"

"She pulled off his mask, anyway."

"And survived." She shivered, then rubbed her upper arms with her hands. "I'll be glad to go back to day shift next week, I can tell you that. How many women has that creep killed now? Six? Seven?"

"Seven." He swore softly, swallowed the last of his coffee and crushed the cup in his fist. "I really thought we had him today."

"You'll get him. At least you've got a witness now."

"Yeah." He lobbed the crumpled cup into the trash can, then glanced at the clock on the wall. "It's been two hours, Lucy. What the hell are they doing to her?"

"CAT scan. An EEG, too, I think. It shouldn't be much longer." She looked at the clock, too, then sighed as she stood up. "Well, back to the trenches."

Then she stood there that one extra, telltale moment, looking at him with those soft blue eyes that held the faintest glimmer of wanting, waiting for him to ask her

what time she got off work or what she was doing next
Saturday night and did she like Chinese or Italian. Hell.
She might just as well have been waiting for him to
recite the Constitution, including the Preamble and all
the damned amendments, backward. He couldn't.

"Take it easy, Luce," he said, and watched that little
glimmer fade to dull disappointment as she turned to
leave.

*I can't, babe.* That's what he should have said. *I just
can't. Not yet.*

No sooner had Lucy left the room than Maggie
O'Connor came in, looking like she'd worked every
single second of their sixteen-hour day. She scowled at
the empty coffeepot.

"Oh, damn. I really needed some of that poison. I'm
about to fall asleep on my feet here."

"There's still some in my thermos out in the car,"
Joe said. "Want me to get it for you?"

"Thanks anyway. There's probably not time.
They're about to take our girl up to a room."

Joe sat up straighter. "Did she come to?"

Maggie shook her head. "But the brain scan didn't
show any damage. Kuhlmann thinks it's a concussion,
that she'll just take a while to come around, probably
with a hell of a headache."

Joe raised an eyebrow. "And a clear memory?"

"I was too tired to ask." She sagged into a chair,
leaned back and put her feet on a magazine-covered
coffee table. "You look a little beat yourself, partner."

"Nah. I was born looking beat. Why don't you go
home, Maggie? I'm going to stick around here, anyway."

"I don't think she's going to come around that fast,
Decker."

"Probably not," he said, "but our masked marvel doesn't know that, does he?"

Maggie opened her eyes wider. "You think he's going to try to pop her? Here? At Saint Cat's?"

Joe shrugged. "I would if I were looking at the electric chair and she was the only one who could ID me. Did you talk to Carson? They get any prints off the vehicles?"

"Just hers all over the Land Cruiser. Our friend was wearing gloves."

"Naturally."

"Oh. I almost forgot." Maggie sat up. "This is hers." She shrugged her shoulder from the leather strap of a large handbag she'd been holding on her lap. "The guys who towed her car found this under the seat."

He reached out for it, nearly dropping the bag once Maggie had let go. "Jesus. What's in here? Bricks?"

Maggie laughed. "It's just a lady's purse. Most of us like to be prepared, you know, Decker."

"For what? Six weeks in the wilderness?"

"Well, you never know." She stood up, stretching, sighing. "Okay. I'm outta here, then. I'll take the car and pick you up in the morning."

"Want me to walk you out, Mag?"

"Nope. There's a gorgeous new guy on security who's just dying to do that. G'night, Decker. Get some sleep, will you?"

He mumbled noncommittally, his hand already in the depths of the black leather handbag, exploring for a wallet. "Bingo." It was a good one—red, made of a soft and supple cowhide. He undid the snap and stared at the driver's license in its little plastic frame. The redhead gazed back at him with her deep-set, round green eyes. Her head was tilted just a little and her mouth, too, as if the camera or its operator amused her. As if she had a secret. A delicious one. Or dangerous.

His gaze moved to the name beneath the photo.

"What do you know, pretty Sara Campbell?" he whispered. "Who did you see?"

Despite the ID he'd discovered in her purse, Joe kept her on the hospital records as a Jane Doe. He walked beside her bed as they wheeled it briskly down the corridor, into an elevator and up to a private room on the sixth floor. He didn't know the floor nurse, a six-foot, two-hundred-pound black drill sergeant whose name tag bore the surprisingly delicate name of Caressa Green.

After she got her patient situated and Joe had made it clear that he wasn't leaving, the big nurse glowered at him from the door. "Don't you be trying to wake her up now and bother her with a bunch of questions. You hear?"

Joe put his hand over his heart. "Trust me, Caressa."

She snorted. "That's Ms. Green to you, Lieutenant." Then she flipped off the overhead light and was gone.

He settled into a chair in the corner of the room. Danish modern, he thought bleakly. Probably to discourage visitors. "It's going to be a long night, pretty Sara," he said softly in the direction of the high bed where her body hardly fleshed out the covers. Her driver's license put her at a hundred fifteen pounds. He thought one ten was probably closer. Maybe even one oh-five.

With a sigh, he returned to exploring the contents of her wallet. If she still lived at 5300 Westbury Boulevard, that meant she was only a few blocks from home when she got hit. He tried to picture the house—mansion, actually, like all the others that sat on their manicured lawns just north of Patriot's Park. So, his Sara wasn't only pretty, she was filthy rich. Chances were good that her family would snatch her out of Saint Cat's and move her to Central Methodist before the sun was up tomorrow. If anybody notified them.

It suddenly occurred to him then that he hadn't checked her hand for a wedding ring. He hesitated a second before he looked and then realized that he was holding his breath, harboring some weird, misguided wish that the fourth finger of her left hand would be ringless, unencumbered. When he saw that it was, he let out his breath and felt his mouth twitching with a goofy little grin.

"Get a grip, Decker," he muttered, going back to his exploration of the chunky red wallet. Miss Sara Campbell would be thirty-one next week, or at least she would be if he had anything to do with it. If she could come through with a solid ID, maybe he'd be able to give her the Ripper's head on a platter for her birthday.

Forty-seven dollars in cash. Visa. MasterCard. Blue Cross/Blue Shield. The suits of Saint Cat's would be plenty relieved to see that, he thought. State Farm. Auto club. A careful girl, his Sara. Zoo membership. Art museum. Public TV. Generous, too. Association of Antique Dealers. Psychiatric Associates—Brendan Bourne, MD. Hmm. Maybe that explained all the plastic prescription vials rattling around in the depths of the bag, as well as the little collapsible cup.

Cell phone. Tampax. Lipstick—Chocolate Silk. Hairbrush. Notebook—blank. A big fat fountain pen. And mints. Six, seven, no, eight rolls of mints, in various stages of consumption. So, his Sara had a sweet tooth, did she? He thought of Edie, forever digging in her hulk of a handbag and coming up with a grin and a linty Life Saver.

"You're going to get hairballs one of these days, baby," he'd warned her, "just like a cat."

Ah, damn. He felt his throat constricting all of a sudden.

He zipped the bag and put it on the floor, then slid down in the chair to rest his head on its inhospitable back. Three years, long ones, and those memories could still catch him unawares, sneaking up and clobbering him with the force of a ball peen hammer. That was one of the reasons he worked the long hours he did. The less time he had for memories, the less he hurt.

The job had always been important to him, but since Edie's death, the job was everything. It was all he had. He'd been a cop for seventeen years, the last ten of those as a detective in Homicide, working his own cases and mopping up the botched cases of guys like Freiheit and Brown—the Geriatric Squad, as they were called behind their backs—who ate doughnuts and watched the clock and counted down the months till their retirement.

The Maniac. That's what they called *him* behind his back and sometimes to his face. It didn't bother him. Not really. Hell, he probably was. Anybody who looked for excuses to hang around the precinct house instead of going home was slightly maniacal, he supposed. The other nickname the guys had for him was Sue, which had nothing to do with his virility but instead was short for suicide. He wasn't suicidal, though.

He'd always taken risks. Now, since Edie was gone, he just took more. That was all.

Joe opened his eyes when he heard soft, rubber-soled footsteps in the doorway. Caressa Green moved toward the bed like a huge, efficient ghost. She leaned over and pointed the beam of a penlight into the Campbell woman's eye.

"How's she doing?" Joe asked quietly.

"The same," she said, talking while she ticked off the beats of the woman's pulse. "She moved any?"

"Nope."

The nurse gave a little cluck of her tongue while she wrote on the chart, then she turned to leave but paused just inside the door. "You want a cot, Lieutenant? A pillow?"

"Why, Caressa." Joe smiled. "I didn't think you cared."

"I just don't want to be treating your sad ass when you wake up with a stiff neck tomorrow."

He chuckled. "A pillow would be nice."

"I'll be right back."

She didn't get far down the corridor, though, before he heard her stern admonishment. "That room's private, mister. You see that sign? No visitors."

"Police," came the reply, and Joe immediately recognized the sandpapery, three-pack-a-day voice of Captain Frank Cobble, his boss. For a guy who put in the shortest hours possible, and most of those at his fussily neat desk, he was up unusually late, Joe thought. He didn't bother to stand or even to straighten up when the captain came into the room.

"Who's there?" Cobble growled, staring across the darkness toward the chair.

"Decker."

"I don't recall assigning any overtime on this."

*Here we go again.* "You didn't, boss. I'm just hanging around here on my own. What brings you out on a night like this?"

"I was at that damn fund-raiser for the mayor. Just thought I'd stop and check on things here before I went home." He moved closer to the bed, angling his head to get a better view in the dim light that filtered in from the corridor. "You got a name for our Jane Doe yet?"

"Campbell, Sara, 5300 Westbury Boulevard."

Cobble's head jerked up. "Campbell? The candy family? That Campbell?"

"Dunno. I figured with that address she was worth at least a mil."

"Try ten or twenty." He looked at Sara, studying her face as if trying to ascertain her exact net worth. "Has she said anything yet? What do the doctors say?"

"That she'll probably come around tomorrow with a beauty of a headache."

"Okay. Well, let me know when she comes around, will you? I'll be at my desk by nine. And don't bother putting in any requests for overtime, Decker. If you want to play hero or bodyguard, you do it on your own time. Understand?"

Joe leaned his head back and closed his eyes. "Right." He would have added "asshole" as Cobble went out the door, but the captain didn't have much of a sense of humor. Not that Joe would have meant it humorously, anyway.

"So you're a candy heiress, pretty Sara," he said softly. "That makes sense. With a sweet face like that."

"Wake up, partner."

Maggie's voice clanged in his head, and Joe opened

one eye just in time to see Caressa Green open the
drapes with a single vicious pull and nearly blind him
with harsh November light. He groaned as he sat upright, trying to work the kinks out of his neck.

"You look like the cat's breakfast, Lieutenant," the
big nurse informed him.

"Meow." Maggie purred unsympathetically as she
put a steaming cup of coffee in his hand. "Drink up.
Our girl looks like she's going to come around pretty
soon. I've got a sketch artist on call just in case she
remembers anything."

He glanced toward the bed to see that its head had
been raised a few degrees. Instead of looking out cold
as she had the night before, Sara Campbell appeared
to be merely sleeping. Then, almost as if he'd wished
it, her eyes blinked open.

"Bingo!" He was out of his chair and bedside in
two seconds flat. "You're awake," he said, trying not
to frighten her any more than she already looked.
"You're in the hospital, Miss Campbell. Saint Catherine's."

Caressa wedged herself between Joe and the bed rail.
"Don't you be hassling her right now, Lieutenant. You
hear me?" She pressed the call button and informed
the nurses' station that her patient was conscious.
"Page that neurology resident, Harker, good and loud.
He's probably sleeping somewhere."

Sara Campbell was gazing around the room like
somebody who'd just awakened on another planet. It
was obvious she didn't know where she was, or why.
How many times had he come to the same way? Joe
wondered. Four, maybe five. But always to Edie's worried face hovering above him and her hand all warm

in his. He took Sara's hand in his and said, "You're going to be just fine, Miss Campbell. I promise."

Her hand clasped his in return, and her green eyes, big with fear, fastened on his face. "Home," she whispered. "I want to go home."

"I want to go home," she said to the doctor who was peeling back her eyelids and aiming the bright beam of a flashlight into her pupils.

"How's the head? Hurt any?" he asked her.

"It's fine." It wasn't, but Sara thought they might not let her go if she confessed that there was a big bass drum between her temples and somebody was beating on it relentlessly. "Really."

"Do you know where you are, Miss Campbell?"

"Saint Catherine's, I think." She glanced at the man who had held her hand so warmly a little while ago. "Isn't that right?"

Her hand holder smiled encouragingly from the window where he had one jeans-clad hip perched on the sill. His gray eyes fastened on her so intensely that it was difficult for her to look away, or even to think, for that matter. When the doctor asked her if she knew what day it was, for a minute Sara wasn't even sure she could come up with the right month.

"Miss Campbell?"

"November," she blurted. "Wasn't yesterday Monday? So this must be Tuesday, the eighth."

He murmured, "That's right," much to her relief, then said, "now can you count backward from twenty for me? By threes?"

"I hate math."

"Do it anyway. Twenty. Seventeen."

Sara let out a little sigh. "Fourteen. Eleven. Um. Eight…"

"Okay. Looks good. All in all, I'd say you're doing a lot better than we expected." He turned toward the window. "She can leave any time, Lieutenant."

"Lieutenant?" Sara looked once more at the man sitting on the windowsill. He stood and kind of sauntered toward her bed.

"I'm Lieutenant Joe Decker, Miss Campbell. This is my partner, Maggie O'Connor. Now that you're better, we'd like to ask you a few questions about what happened yesterday."

Yesterday. Sara tried to make her brain cut through the infernal clamor of the drumbeat inside her head. Yesterday. Yes, she remembered. She had told Dr. Bourne she was going home for good. She had driven home in the rain. Only… Only she never got there. Her heart took a sudden extra beat, and she could feel the prickle of panic beginning.

"I just want to go home." She swung her legs out from under the covers and started to get out of the high bed, but the lieutenant's hand clasped her shoulder.

"Whoa, now. You might want to wait just a minute here. Maggie, are her clothes in the closet?"

"They're in here." The big nurse came forward, opened a drawer and took out a plastic bag. "She'll have to sign for those. The release form's taped on the other side." She tossed it onto the bed.

Only then did Sara realize why the man had stopped her. She was wearing only a thin cotton hospital gown, probably pure daylight in the back. Or if not daylight, then a very full moon. She wished she could think more clearly. But she would, once she got home.

"We'll wait outside," he said. "After you're

dressed, we'll drive you home. We can question you there. Come on, Maggie.''

"Question me?" Sara murmured once they were gone.

The nurse picked up a handbag from the floor. "This yours?''

Sara nodded, accepting the handbag, enjoying its familiar weight. "Why do they need to question me? What in the world about?''

"You don't remember the accident you were in?''

"Well, sure." She frowned, once more aware of the static inside her head. "Well, sort of. Vaguely. It was raining and there was a stalled car and then…bam!''

The nurse shrugged. "Well, I guess it's that bam they want to find out a little more about. I don't know. All I know is that lieutenant stuck to you like glue all through the night.''

"Did he?" Sara blinked. She couldn't imagine being in the same room with a man like that and not being aware of him, even if she was unconscious. It made her feel uncomfortable but at the same time oddly safe.

"Uh-huh. Now let's get you dressed so you can go home.''

"Oh, yes. Please.''

The woman's knuckles had been a pearly white on the arms of the wheelchair all the way from her room to the rear exit of the hospital, and she appeared just as ill at ease in the car, maybe more so, but that was understandable, Joe thought, since the last time Sara Campbell had been in a car somebody had crashed into her and then assaulted her. He didn't wish the woman unpleasant memories, but the more she remembered, the easier his job would be and the sooner the Ripper would be on his way to the chair.

Maggie dropped them off at the big house on Westbury Boulevard. She was going on to the tow lot downtown to retrieve Sara Campbell's car and keys. Once the redhead was out of the car and standing on her own sidewalk, she seemed to relax a little. When Joe asked her if she had a spare house key, it was the first time he'd heard her laugh. A rich alto with husky undertones. Just like her voice.

"A spare, Lieutenant? I have a spare, an auxiliary spare, a son of spare and a few more. Can you tell I don't like to be locked out of my house?"

The one she came up with wasn't all that well hidden, in his estimation, in a dead-giveaway wrought-iron turtle by the front door. When he snickered that no thief would ever think to look there, she started looking so distressed that Joe immediately regretted his remark, and added, "Hey, what self-respecting thief would use the front door anyway?"

He followed her into a two-story marble and gilt foyer, and he must have sucked in his breath or given some other indication that it reminded him of an art museum or the Rotunda of the Capitol in D.C. because Sara Campbell immediately said, "It's a little gaudy, isn't it? I've pretty much kept to the back of the house ever since my parents died last winter." She shrugged and offered him the smallest of smiles. "Come on. Follow me."

He did, down a long, polished, paneled hallway along which the cream-colored carpet sank a good two inches under his feet, and Joe became uncharacteristically concerned about the wet soles of his boots and the jeans and flannel shirt he'd worn since yesterday morning. Money was one thing. Edie's family had had money. But this much wealth was, well, almost institutional. Who'd ever think there was such profit in candy bars and all-day suckers?

"This is nice," he said, feeling he had to say something. The place kind of demanded it.

"This is nicer." Sara turned right, shrugged off her trench coat and tossed that along with her handbag onto an enormous leather couch. "God, it's good to be home," she said with a long, deep sigh.

It *was* nicer, Joe thought as he looked around. While the rest of the house fairly screamed money and lots of it, this room whispered total comfort from its book-lined walls to its big brick fireplace and dark peg-and-plank floors. The shutters on the windows were the same dark wood. Sara turned on a lamp, and its mellow light further burnished all the rich patinas inside the cozy space.

"Have a seat, Lieutenant Decker." She gestured toward a muted plaid club chair that looked big enough for two. "I'm dying for a cup of coffee. Would you like some? Or some tea?"

There was a note of confidence in her voice that he hadn't heard before either at the hospital or in the car. All the frown lines on her forehead had smoothed out, and her tense mouth had relaxed to the point where it appeared almost sensual. So sensual Joe had to pull his gaze away.

"Coffee would be nice, thanks."

"Good. I'll be right back." She shivered slightly and rubbed her upper arms. "It's a little chilly in here. If you'd like to light a fire, the matches are just to the right of the hearth."

After the kindling crackled and the pine logs began

to blaze, Joe leaned back in the chair, staring into the flames, trying not to remember other winters, other fires, especially ones in the ramshackle Victorian where he'd been so happy. During the last three years, he'd been pretty successful in fending off all those memories, but they were making a hell of a comeback now, and he didn't like that one bit.

He snatched a magazine from a stack on the coffee table and began to thumb through it in search of a distraction. It was a bad choice, he realized, when page after page of pouty lips and lithe limbs flashed before his eyes. He tossed it on the table, wondering, where was *Field and Stream* when he needed it?

"Lieutenant?"

Sara Campbell's face appeared in the doorway, smiling for no particular reason Joe could imagine other than making him want to smile almost sappily in return.

"The coffee's on," she said. "Give me two minutes to take a shower and change, all right?"

"Take all the time you need," Joe said with a sigh, fairly certain that she would anyway, and not all that reluctant to enjoy the warmth of the fire and to savor the peacefulness of this room a little while longer. Well, hell. The Ripper had been at it for nearly a year and a half. He didn't suppose another hour or two would make all that much difference.

"What do you mean, you don't remember?" Joe clicked his ballpoint pen closed, then clicked it open again.

"I don't remember."

"Let's try this again, Miss Campbell. The pickup hit your left front fender. The guy jumped out. He opened your door and grabbed you. Pulled you out of your vehicle.''

''Yes. I remember that.''

''And?''

''I screamed. I struggled. I remember hitting him and trying to scratch him, only there was no place to scratch because of his coat and gloves and that mask.''

''Right. Then you pulled off the mask.''

''Yes. There was a kind of tassel on the top, and I grabbed it as hard as I could.'' She took a sip of her coffee and put the cup in the saucer with deliberation. ''Everything's a blur after that, Lieutenant. I'm sorry.''

Joe clicked his pen again and recrossed his legs. *Blur* wasn't going to cut it, dammit. He was usually a better interrogator than this, but he kept getting distracted by the geography of Sara Campbell. She'd changed out of a loose tunic into a black wool turtleneck that fit her like a wet suit and a pair of jeans that might as well have been denim skin. Ordinarily he didn't notice women's clothes, but ordinarily clothes didn't curve and swell and sway the way Sara Campbell's did.

Her hair was damp from her shower, framing her freshly scrubbed face in soft auburn curls and brushing against the high neck of her sweater. She looked good in black, he thought. Edible. Like licorice.

He cleared his throat. ''You looked at him after you yanked the mask off, right? Before he slugged you?''

''I must've looked at him,'' she said.

''And? Dark? Light? Mustache? Anything?''

She shook her head. ''Nothing.''

He put the pen in his shirt pocket and let his notebook flop closed. The little growl that issued from his throat was one of frustration, but it made the woman wince.

"I'm sorry," she said again, drawing her feet beneath her and retreating further into the pillowed corner of the big couch. She gazed at the fire a second, then at him. "Look. I know the accident was his fault. I know he assaulted me. But I'd just as soon forget it ever happened. You don't have to arrest him, Lieutenant. I have no intention of pressing charges."

Leaning his head back, Joe closed his eyes and let out a long breath. Okay. He hadn't wanted to frighten her, but maybe that was unavoidable. "Are you familiar with the Ripper, Miss Campbell?" he asked quietly.

"Sure. Who isn't?"

He straightened, leaned forward with his elbows on his knees and fixed her with the most intense gaze, the most grim expression he knew how to muster. "I think that was him. Yesterday. The guy in the ski mask."

Her eyes grew a little wider, and her mouth tensed. Otherwise, she held absolutely still. "What are you saying?"

"That we've been chasing a phantom killer for nearly eighteen months, and until yesterday, nobody— nobody but his victims—had ever seen his face."

She stared at him, her green eyes growing wider, her breath quickening a little, her lips compressing into a pale line.

"You saw him. When you pulled off that mask, you saw his face."

"But I didn't!"

He kept his voice level but insistent. "You saw him."

"I don't know," she wailed. "Oh, God. Maybe I did. Maybe. But I just don't remember."

"Just close your eyes a minute and try."

Her green eyes disappeared behind long, dark lashes,

giving Joe an opportunity to let his eyes freely and boldly survey each and every curve of black wool and faded denim. He should have felt guilty. Like a Peeping Tom. But he didn't. There was no malice in his gaze, and God knew there was no intent of harm or anything else. He was just taking in the view. An enchanted tourist in Sara Campbell's corner of the world.

The weather must have taken another cold turn because, while he gazed at Sara, he heard sleet pattering on the windows and wind slapping at a shutter somewhere. The sounds of the storm made the room feel all the more cozy, and suddenly he dreaded leaving, going back to the station house and inevitably to his cold, spare apartment with its unmade pullout bed that hadn't seen its sofa incarnation since he'd first wrestled it open nearly three years ago.

While Sara, behind closed eyes, tried to conjure up the face of the Ripper, Joe found himself trying to imagine the bed where she slept. It would have to be even more cozy and inviting than this. A big bed. Maybe brass. With a comforter as thick as a pillow, but weightless all the same. Soft white sheets where her fragrance lingered, and her warmth...

The pager on his belt emitted a harsh series of beeps, jerking open his eyes and putting an end to his reverie. It was just as well, he thought while he unclipped the little black box and read the message in its window. Maggie. Back to business.

Sara Campbell's eyes were open, too. The sudden beeps had brought her bolt upright on the couch.

"May I use your phone?" Joe asked.

"Sure." She pointed to the rolltop desk on the opposite side of the room. "It's right over there." She stood and reached for her cup and saucer. "I think I'll have a refill. Can I bring you some?"

"No, thanks." As he started punching numbers into the phone, he decided not to bother telling Sara that he doubted she'd have time to drink that second cup.

Sara stood at the kitchen sink, gazing into the back yard where sleet pelted the red bricks on the patio and weighed heavily on the limbs of the big blue spruce. Her headache had subsided to a nagging little throb. She rolled her neck, testing the stiffness there, finding that it, too, had eased.

God, it was good to be home, she thought, even if her homecoming had been delayed by 18 hours or so. The accident and the subsequent detour to the hospital only made her savor her sanctuary more. Once Lieutenant Decker was gone, she'd make that long-overdue grilled cheese sandwich and uncork the bottle of Merlot to celebrate.

Or, she thought, maybe she'd invite him to stay and have lunch with her. It was nearly ten-thirty, and she doubted if he'd had any breakfast. Of course, if he was on duty, the wine was probably out of the question, even if he did strike her as somebody who didn't necessarily play by the rules. She always thought homicide detectives were middle-aged men who wore suits and ties rather than thirtyish hunks in jeans and flannel shirts. Joe Decker looked more like a lumberjack than a cop.

Not that she'd ever seen a lumberjack, she thought, turning from the window to fill her cup. Not that she'd seen the infamous Ripper, either. When she searched her brain, no face came into focus. She could see the ski mask, even feel its wet navy wool on her fingertips.

But the face simply refused to materialize no matter how hard she tried.

Lieutenant Decker was still on the phone when she returned to the den so she scooted into her corner of the couch and sipped her coffee, idly perusing him— okay, ogling—while he sat at the rolltop desk, seemingly unaware of her return. His hair was longish, a light brown shot through with just a hint of gray, making Sara revise her estimate of his age to forty, plus or minus two. When he turned a little to his right, she could see his profile, which included a jaw that looked like granite and a nose that looked like it wasn't quite that hard and had been broken a time or two. Football, she speculated. No, soccer. His jeans, rather than disguise his legs, seemed to emphasize the bunched muscles of his thighs and the long, strong muscles of his calves. He'd look great in shorts.

Her gaze drifted over the leather shoulder holster he wore. It seemed more sexy than dangerous. She couldn't hear his conversation, but she tuned in to the deep baritone of his voice. That was sexy, too. Then it stopped. He put the phone in its cradle and swiveled in the chair as if he knew she'd been there all along.

"That was Maggie. She'll be here in a few minutes with your keys. The Land Cruiser wasn't driveable, so she had them tow it to the dealership for repairs. She figured that's what you'd want."

"That's fine," Sara said. They could keep it for all she cared. Maybe she'd call them later and see how much they'd give her for it.

"I'm sure they can arrange for you to have a loaner while they're working on it."

Sara nodded, thinking it was sweet that the lieutenant was concerned about her transportation or lack of it.

Maybe she would ask if he wanted a grilled cheese sandwich and a glass of Merlot, after all. No. His partner was on her way. There wasn't time.

He glanced at his watch, then stood up. A sudden vision of soccer shorts made Sara smile as she watched him walk around the back of the other couch. She felt a tiny pang when he picked up his leather jacket and shrugged into it. But then he picked up her trench coat, holding it up, open.

"Ready?" he asked.

Sara blinked. Ready? "For what?"

"We're taking you down to the station house to go through some mug shots."

It only took a second for her heart to start pounding and her hands to get clammy and that feeling of panic to rise in her throat like an inaudible scream. Then Sara remembered her plan. She took in a deep breath and let it out slowly before she said, "I'd rather not."

Now it was Decker who blinked. "Excuse me?"

"I said I'd rather not, Lieutenant."

# Chapter 3

His eyes narrowed, and a muscle jerked in his cheek. Decker was obviously used to calling the shots, Sara thought, and he probably didn't even know the meaning of the word no. Well, he was about to get an education. She wasn't going to leave her house. Period. That thought alone was enough to slow her racing heart and to keep her from breaking out in a cold sweat.

He was holding her trench coat almost fiercely, the way a matador holds his cape before a bull. "You'd rather not," he muttered.

"That's what I said."

"Okay. Well…" He shook his head slightly, then draped her coat over the back of the couch. "I guess it doesn't have to be right now. I can come back for you later this afternoon. Four o'clock? How does that sound?"

"Terrible," she said, crossing her arms.

"Well, you give me a time, then, Miss Campbell."

It was almost a shout, but not quite. The more annoyed Decker became with her, the more Sara relaxed, the more she reveled in her ability to say no. She hadn't been completely sure of her resolve yesterday when she'd announced her plan to Dr. Bourne. But suddenly she knew she wasn't going to cave in to other people's demands. She was free. Truly. It felt almost like having wings!

"I don't want to go to the police station at all. If you'd like to bring the photographs here, Lieutenant Decker, I'll be happy to look at them."

"That's against regulations." His eyebrows were almost touching as he scowled at her. "What about tomorrow if you don't want to go today?"

"I don't want to go *ever.*"

He rolled his eyes and practically growled at her. "I don't understand."

"Have you ever heard of agoraphobia, Lieutenant?"

"No," he snarled. "What's that? Fear of fuzzy sweaters?"

"Oh, that's cute. No, it isn't. It's what I have. I have panic attacks when I leave my house. So I'm never leaving my house again. Ever!"

He stared at her as if she'd grown a third eye, a second nose and an additional mouth. One that was frothing. "That's crazy!"

This time he did shout, so Sara shouted back. "It is *not* crazy, you jerk. It's just neurotic."

When Maggie honked a few minutes later to announce her arrival, Joe stalked out to the car. He nearly wrenched the door handle off getting in, then slammed the door with such vengeance that his partner almost spilled her large paper cup of coffee.

"Jeez, Decker. What's with you?"

"Not our witness, that's for sure." He swore and slapped the dashboard with his open hand. "She won't come to the station house. Ever!"

"What do you mean—ever?"

"Well, Mag, I guess I mean never, no way, not in a million years and over her dead body. That pretty well sums it up."

Maggie took a sip of coffee. "What the hell did you say to make her so angry?"

"She's not angry, dammit. She's nuts."

"She seemed pretty sane to me."

"Ha!" He hunkered down in the passenger seat, hitting his knees against the dash, swearing again.

Maggie turned off the engine with a sigh. "Did she come up with any kind of description of our guy?"

"No."

"Then she has to come look at the books. Did you explain it to her?"

"She wants us to bring the books to her."

"We can't do that. It's against regulations." She gave a snort, glaring at the huge house. "Who does this Campbell woman think she is, anyway? The Queen?"

"The queen of nuts," he muttered. "She says she's got... Aw, hell. What was it? Ag-something. Agoraphobia."

"Aw, jeez," she said softly.

Joe twisted his head toward her. "What? You've heard of it?"

Maggie nodded. "Yeah, I have, actually. I have an aunt who hasn't been out of her house in nearly a dozen years. She used to be able to come to my mom's for

Thanksgiving and Christmas, but now she can't even do that.''

''Oh, great.''

''Poor Aunt Rose. She couldn't even go to her daughter's wedding.''

''Couldn't or wouldn't?'' Joe snapped, but at the same time he was remembering the look of fear on Sara Campbell's face when he'd told her it was time to go. Still, he couldn't even pretend to understand. Panicking when a masked man wrestles you from a car was one thing, but to panic over walking out your own front door didn't make any sense to him.

Maggie lodged her cup on the center console and unfastened her seat belt. ''I'll go talk to her. You stay here and sulk, Decker. You probably scared her half to death, anyway.''

He rolled his window down and yelled to her as she made her way up the slippery walk. ''Don't take no for an answer, Mag. She's got to look at those pictures.''

Sara opened the front door, partly relieved to see it was Sergeant Maggie O'Connor standing there, but wary all the same, especially when she glimpsed Lieutenant Decker glowering at her from the passenger side of the car. His breath was coming out in a cloud that looked like hot steam. She invited the woman in, then waited for the usual, rather breathless, silly comments about the magnificence of the foyer. She should just have people come to the back door, she thought, to avoid all the fuss.

But the sergeant seemed oblivious of the marble and gilt that surrounded her and kept her gaze on Sara. ''Joe explained the problem, Miss Campbell,'' she said without preamble. "Is there anything I can do to re-assure you? This shouldn't take long. We could have you back here in an hour or less."

"I can't." Sara felt tears welling in her eyes. She wasn't used to talking about her problem. She was used to offering lame excuses rather than the truth. And she wasn't all that used to saying no. "I know you think I'm being uncooperative, but I'm not. Really. Can't you bring the photographs here?"

"Look. It's okay. I understand." The sergeant put her hand on Sara's arm and squeezed gently. "I mean, as much as anybody can understand. My aunt Rose has the same problem. Have you got any tranquilizers around? Maybe if you took a couple…"

Sara shook her head. "They don't help."

"Okay."

Maggie O'Connor chewed her lower lip a moment as if trying to come up with a solution while Sara stood there, steeling herself to say no for what felt like the thousandth time. But then the sergeant grinned quite unexpectedly.

"We'll be back in about an hour with the pictures, okay?"

"I thought the lieutenant said that was against regulations."

"It is," she said, "but the lieutenant has a reputation of bending those when he has to. And I guess this is just one of those cases, isn't it?"

Sara felt herself breathing again, drawing cool air and sweet relief deep into her lungs. "Thank you, Sergeant."

"That's okay." Maggie O'Connor's gaze intensified on Sara's face. "Look. It really isn't any of my business, but I'm probably not doing you any favors in the long run, Miss Campbell. I guess you already know that.''

"I only know you're doing me a huge favor now, and I appreciate it more than I can say."

Joe hadn't seen the top of his desk in months. It was such a mess that the captain had had it moved to a far corner of the squad room, which was fine with Joe because he didn't have as far to go to get a cup of coffee. Frank Cobble was eyeballing his desk right now, as if he wished he could move it even farther away. Like Siberia.

"How's it going with the Campbell woman?" he asked as he flipped the pages of Joe's desk calendar two weeks forward to the correct day. "Did you get anything in the way of a description yet?"

"We're working on it," Joe answered, sliding the manila envelope crammed with borrowed mug shots into his top drawer. All innocence, he looked at his boss's narrowed eyes and pinched mouth. "What about some kind of security for her, Captain?"

"No can do, Decker. I told you last night. No more overtime until the new budget makes it through the city council." The captain picked up a pen half buried under papers, then scrutinized the desktop. "You got a cap for this, Decker? These cheap pens run dry overnight if you don't cap them."

Joe sighed. He didn't think much of Frank Cobble to begin with, but the man's ability to focus on the insignificant and the inane practically made the fillings ache in Joe's clenched teeth. "I'll get right on that, Captain."

Maggie was sauntering across the squad room, licking the cream filling from a doughnut off her fingers.

"It's a little late for breakfast, isn't it, O'Connor?" Cobble snapped.

"This is lunch," Maggie answered matter-of-factly, causing the captain to roll his eyes and retreat to the safety of his pristine office. "Did you get them?" she whispered, perching on the edge of Joe's desk.

He opened the drawer a few inches, disclosing the manila envelope. "Let's just hope our guy's in there."

"And that Sara Campbell can ID him."

"Yeah. And that he can't ID her. Which reminds me." Joe mounted his most effective grin. "What are you doing tonight, Mag?"

"Oh, no." Maggie jumped up as if the desktop had suddenly turned red hot. "Uh-uh. I've finally got a date with that security guard at Saint Cat's. No way am I going to cancel."

He threw up his hands. "Well, what the hell are we going to do, then? I can't quite see the Princess of Panic agreeing to go to a hotel, can you?"

"Can't Cobble assign somebody?"

Joe swore. "He's too busy worrying about putting caps on pens and the red ink in the budget to worry about the only witness in this case." He picked up a pen, wrenched off its cap and hurled them both across the room.

"Well, then, I guess you're in the bodyguard business again, Decker." She waggled her eyebrows. "At least for another night."

When the doorbell rang, Sara was just pulling her perfectly browned grilled cheese sandwich from under the broiler. Startled by the bell, she dropped the gooey concoction on the floor, and then, when she tried to pick it up, the melted cheese stuck like molten lava to her thumb. She headed down the long hall to the front door, alternately flipping on lights and sucking her thumb as she went. The bell rang once more before she got there.

"All right. I'm coming. I'm coming," she muttered, then called out, "who's there?"

"Joe Decker," came the deep baritone reply from the opposite side of the door.

Sara paused, one hand on the lock, the other on the knob, her thumb beginning to throb and her inner panic alarm starting to sound its warning. "You're not going to try to cart me off someplace, are you, Lieutenant? Because, if you are, you're really wasting your time."

"Open the door, Miss Campbell."

He sounded just as annoyed as when he'd left a few hours ago. Sara opened the door, expecting to see a grim set to his ruggedly handsome face, but he was grinning instead and holding up a big envelope.

"Pictures," he said, stepping across the threshold. "Time to play pin the tail on the perp."

Her heart skipped a little beat, and it took her a second to realize that the sensation wasn't from anxiety, but rather from the surprising sight of the crinkles in the corners of his steel gray eyes and the sudden slash of his smile. They took her breath away for a moment. Not knowing what to say or how to say it, Sara popped her thumb in her mouth again.

"What did you do," he asked, "burn yourself on a grilled cheese sandwich?"

Sara felt her eyes almost bug out. She pulled her thumb away. "How did you know that?"

"I'm a detective, remember?" He laughed, and his eyes crinkled even more.

"I'm serious. How in the world did you know that?"

He tapped the side of his nose. "Eau de grilled cheese." Then he jammed the envelope under his arm and took her hand in both of his. "It's blistering. We should probably get some antibiotic cream on that."

His hands were warm, which seemed amazing since he'd just come in from the cold. His voice was gentle, which was even more amazing since the last time she'd seen him he'd yelled that she was crazy.

"I'm sorry I called you a jerk, Lieutenant," she said. "You know. Before. When you called me..."

"A nutcase?" He smiled while his thumb traced along hers.

"Crazy, I believe, was the exact word."

"Oh, yeah. Well, I guess I was a jerk, then."

She tipped her face to his. That grin of his was irresistible, and she felt her mouth being tugged at the corners. "Is that an apology, then?"

"That's about as close as I ever get."

She laughed out loud. "Then I guess I better accept it." It wasn't easy to take her eyes off him or withdraw her hand from his grasp, but she did. "What about these pictures?"

He looked at the envelope tucked under his arm as if he'd completely forgotten it was there. "Oh, these. They can wait a few minutes. Let's take care of that burn first, okay?"

They were in the little powder room off the kitchen, Decker with one hip angled on the vanity, Sara perched on the closed commode with her arm draped across the lieutenant's leg. In such close quarters she was more than a little aware of the heat from his muscular body, not to mention the wonderfully tropical, almost edible scent of his cologne.

While his head was bent over her hand, she perused
the strands of silver in his hair and studied the way it
curled softly over the collar of his flannel shirt. Nice,
she thought. Too nice.

"This is silly," she said, trying to suppress a nervous laugh. "I can do this myself, you know."

"Hold still." His baritone dropped to a soft growl.
"Where did you get your medical degree, Campbell?"

"Well, where did you get yours, Decker?"

"Premed," he said, tearing the wrapper off a Band-
Aid. "And prelaw. Right here at the university. I quit
after one year of law school. Turn your hand the other
way."

Sara did as she was told. "Why'd you quit?"

"Well..." He positioned the vinyl strip carefully
over her thumb. "It seemed pretty clear that my wife
was going to make a better lawyer than I was, so I got
a job to put her the rest of the way through school."
He pressed the ends of the bandage to her finger.
"There. All done. I don't think we'll have to ampu-
tate."

"Oh," she said, feeling stupid and disappointed and
inexplicably sad all at once. "So your wife's a lawyer.
You must make quite a team."

"We did. She died three years ago."

"I'm so sorry," Sara breathed.

"So am I."

He stood up, letting go of her hand. There was a
kind of half smile on his face, a woeful, little-boy-lost
expression that touched Sara's heart. It was all she
could do not to press the palm of her hand to his cheek.
The intensity of her desire to comfort him fairly
shocked her.

Well, there was comfort and then there was comfort food, she thought.

"Would you like a grilled cheese sandwich, Lieutenant?"

The kitchen was practically as cozy as the den with its light oak glass-fronted cabinets and bright Mediterranean tiles. Joe settled on a rush-seated stool, leaned his elbows on the center island and watched Sara Campbell, or more exactly Sara Campbell's shapely derriere, while she muttered to herself and pawed through the refrigerator, every once in a while tossing something—a loaf of bread, a stick of butter, a package of cheese—onto the adjacent countertop. It had been a long time since he'd enjoyed the sight of a woman fussing in a kitchen.

"Two sandwiches, Lieutenant?" she asked.

"Sounds good."

Her hands were graceful, he noticed, and her movements deft and sure, which surprised him a little considering her condition or her affliction or whatever the hell it was. She didn't strike him as a nervous Nellie at all, but a woman who was cool and calm and completely secure. He liked watching her. Probably more than he should have, he was quick to remind himself, when his gaze kept straying from her face and busy hands to that shapely backside and those equally shapely breasts. His body, running ahead of his brain, had already responded to those curves. Now, *that* hadn't happened in a long, long time.

She hummed the refrain from a golden oldie, sweetly off-key, while she lined up the buttered sandwiches on a metal pan. "Let's see if I can do this without grilling myself this time," she said with a little laugh, opening the wall oven and sliding the pan under the red heating element.

The phone on the far wall rang, and Sara glanced at it, frowning, then at the oven.

Joe stood up. "Go ahead. I'll watch them." He reached out for the spatula she was clasping.

"Thanks."

She hurried around the island and caught the phone on the fourth ring, said a bright hello, followed it a moment later with a more insistent one, then put the receiver back. "Odd," she said. "There was somebody there, but they didn't say anything. Oh, well." She walked to where Joe was standing guard at the oven. "I'll take over now, Lieutenant."

"Do you have caller ID, Miss Campbell?" he asked, handing over the spatula.

"Uh-huh. The box is in the den. Why?"

He shrugged. "Nothing important, really. I just thought I'd take a look at it. Do you mind?"

"No. Not at all. The den's…"

"I'll find it."

He deliberately ambled out of the kitchen, then walked a little faster to the cozy, firelit room where he'd been earlier that day. The phone and the ID box were on the rolltop desk, and Joe wasn't all that surprised to see that the call Sara Campbell had just received had come from a pay phone. He wrote the number down and shoved it in his pocket, cursing softly. It was time to check the windows and doors on the first floor.

"I kept your sandwiches warm," Sara said when he finally got back to the kitchen. "I went ahead with mine. I was starving."

"Sorry. I had to make a couple of phone calls."

"Did you see who that was on the phone earlier?"

"Just somebody trying to sell you a subscription to the paper," Joe lied. He didn't want to frighten her, even though she was going to have to know sooner or later that she wasn't safe in this monster of a house with its scores of mullioned windows and half a dozen French doors with inferior locks.

She slid a plate in front of him with two gorgeous sandwiches flanked by a pickle, a pepper and a few of those midget ears of corn. God, he was famished. But he'd already wasted too much time enjoying Sara Campbell rather than interrogating her, so instead of digging into the food, he got up and retrieved the manila envelope he'd left with his coat. He tossed it onto her side of the island as he sat down.

"Pictures," he said. "Remember? Let's hope you see a familiar face."

She stared at the envelope for a second, then opened it cautiously as if she expected it to explode. She pulled out the stack of vinyl photo sleeves, sighed and said, "Okay. Here goes."

Joe bit into the sandwich and wanted to moan from the pure pleasure of it. Nothing had ever tasted so good. At least not in the past three years. He ate slowly, savoring each bite, and watched Sara's eyes move from picture to picture, from page to page, before they lifted to meet his.

She shook her head. "Nothing. None of them looks the least bit familiar." She added a breathy little, "Thank God."

"I wasn't holding out too much hope that our guy was in there, anyway." He wiped his mouth and hands with a blue-checkered napkin, folded it neatly, then tucked it beneath the empty plate. "I don't suppose there's any way I could get you to check into a hotel under an assumed name, is there?''

"No," she answered, beginning to look wary again. "Why on earth would you want me to go to a hotel?"

"Because you're not safe here," he told her bluntly. "I don't know if you've thought about this, but the Ripper not only knows you can identify him, he can identify you, too."

Her lips twitched a little and she sat up straighter. "No, I hadn't thought about that. You mean you think he'll come after me?"

"It's possible."

"But he doesn't know who I am," she protested.

"I'm betting that finding out who you are is right at the top of his to-do list." He didn't add his suspicion that the creep probably already had found out and had called her from the pay phone whose number was in his shirt pocket. He'd have somebody follow up on that tomorrow, but he already knew they wouldn't find any good prints. "If you went to a hotel…"

"I wasn't kidding when I said I didn't intend to leave my house again, Lieutenant." She crossed her arms. "Really. I meant it. And I still do." Her green eyes narrowed with suspicion. "You can't *make* me go to a hotel, can you?"

"I wish I could," he said with a mournful laugh. "But since you won't, somebody's going to have to stay with you."

"Who?"

"Me. Tonight, anyway."

"Oh."

"Is that all right with you?" he asked, knowing he couldn't stay without her permission, hoping she didn't know that, that if she said get out, he'd have to, and then he'd find himself spending a long, cold and cramped night in his car out front.

It worried him when she seemed to be deliberating too long, but then she picked up his empty plate, carried it to the sink and over her shoulder said, "I guess so, Lieutenant. As long as I get to stay home, that's just fine with me."

# Chapter 4

Sara put two more logs on the fire while she waited for Joe Decker to come in from his car. She'd offered to let him pull the ancient Mustang out of the nasty weather and into the garage, but he'd declined. "It's better if it looks like you've got company," he'd told her.

Better for what? she wondered. It was all a little difficult to believe, Sara thought as she curled into her habitual corner of the couch and sipped the Merlot she'd meant to have last night. She didn't feel threatened by the Ripper or anybody else. She was home, after all. This was her sanctuary. She thought that Lieutenant Decker was probably overreacting, but then she decided she was glad that he was. The thought made her smile. It was nice having somebody worried about her. Somebody other than herself for a change. Even if it was, she reminded herself, just professional.

He came into the den, snow in his hair and his teeth

clenched against the cold. "It's freezing out there," he said, shrugging out of his leather jacket.

"Come warm up by the fire."

"Good idea." He held up a small canvas bag. "Mind if I stash my stuff in the bathroom off the kitchen?"

"That's fine."

"Be right back."

While he was gone, Sara traced her index finger around the rim of her wineglass and tried not to think about the last time she'd spent an evening in this room with a man. Those thoughts, however, weren't so easily denied.

It had been a cold night, just like this one, almost a year ago to the day, when Carter McKay had arrived to take her to the Beaux Arts Ball, the annual open house and formal dance for the art museum. Her parents were out of town, but since they were fairly substantial contributors, Sara was obliged to attend in their absence. Only she hadn't wanted to go. Really hadn't wanted to go. Dreaded it, in fact.

Even now, a year later, she couldn't come up with a reason she had felt that twinge of panic while she dressed for the affair. The weather had been bad, just like tonight, but Carter was a good driver and the museum, in Patriot's Park, wasn't all that far away. Her gown, a deep blue satin moiré, was divine. It was even a good hair day. But by the time Carter arrived, she had managed to tie her stomach in a tangle of knots and to work herself up into a full-fledged, clammy-handed, heart-thumping tizzy.

"Why don't we just stay home?" she'd asked, hiding her inexplicable terror beneath a cool facade. "We

could light a fire, Carter. Close all the blinds. Make
love on Mother's new Aubusson rug.''

"We can do that afterward," he'd replied rather
brusquely as he held up her long black velvet coat.
"We're already late, Sara. Let's go."

"I'm not feeling all that well."

It wasn't a lie, yet it was. She felt ill enough to toss
her cookies right that minute at the prospect of having
to go to the party, yet at the same time, she knew she'd
recover immediately if he'd just agreed to stay home.

He had agreed, grudgingly. But after he'd sulked and
whined and generally made her feel as if she'd ruined
not just his night, but his entire life, Sara had insisted
that he go, if only to enjoy the final hour or so of the
party. And to her amazement, once he was gone, she
felt calm and content and...well...free.

"I like this room."

The lieutenant's voice startled her. She'd been so
lost in thought and the depths of her wineglass that she
hadn't been aware of his return.

"Thank you. I do, too." She gestured toward the
chair on the opposite side of the coffee table. "Well,
make yourself comfortable, Lieutenant. If you'd like a
glass of wine..."

He shook his head as he settled into the big club
chair. "You don't have to treat me like a guest, Miss
Campbell. In fact, it's okay if you want to consider me
just a piece of furniture." He grinned that lopsided but
lethal grin of his, making Sara wonder what kind of
furniture was so perfectly upholstered in denim and
flannel that it was nearly impossible to look away.

She glanced at the clock on the rolltop desk. It was
only seven-thirty, a mere twelve hours since she'd
awakened in the hospital. It felt like a month or more.

All of a sudden she felt bone tired. As if to confirm it, her jaws contracted in a yawn she wasn't quick enough to stifle.

"Sorry," she said. "It's been a long day."

"How's your head?"

She reached up to feel the tender bump just above her ear. "Not bad. I'm sorry I wasn't more help with those pictures. I hope you don't get in any trouble for bringing them here."

He shrugged, as if getting in trouble was something he did on a daily basis. "No problem. Why don't you go to bed if you're tired? You don't have to entertain me. As I said, Miss Campbell, just consider me a piece of furniture."

She smiled. "You're the first piece of furniture I've seen wearing a gun. The first person, actually."

"I can take it off if it bothers you."

"No. Just the opposite, actually." She tucked her legs a little farther beneath her. "It makes me feel safe."

"You should probably think about getting one if you intend to keep living here. I mean, even after we put this Ripper guy behind bars."

"I don't know. Knowing me, I'd be shaking so hard that I'd wind up shooting myself instead of an intruder."

"I could teach you," he said. "If you wanted."

"Maybe. Anyway, I doubt if I'll be living here all that much longer."

He raised a curious eyebrow. "Too much space?"

"Too much money." When his face registered surprise, she continued. "My parents liked to live well. I guess this house pretty well describes their life-style. Grand, just this side of gaudy. Anyway, when they died this past January, there really wasn't anything left except this house, and I had to refinance just to get the mortgage payments down somewhere below the level of the national debt.'' She took another sip of wine, then chuckled. "Poor little rich girl, huh?"

"I'm sorry about your parents. I read about that in the paper."

"It kind of threw me for a loop. One day they were all smiles, all excited about getting out of here and spending the rest of the winter in Bermuda. The next day their plane was missing and presumed lost. Poof. They were gone. Just like that.'' As she snapped her fingers, Sara felt that too familiar lump creep into her throat and tears begin to well in her eyes. "Sorry," she said with a sniff.

"That's okay. I'd offer you that old cliché about time healing these things, but you've probably already heard that a thousand times and haven't believed it once. I know I didn't."

She was just about to ask him how his wife had died when the phone screeched across the room. Sara unwound her legs and began to get up, but Lieutenant Decker was on his feet first. He walked to the desk and peered at the caller ID box while the phone continued to ring.

"Goddammit," he swore. "How the hell did Cormack get wind of this?"

Sara was beside him, not knowing whether to pick up the receiver or not. "Cormack? Who?"

"From the *Daily Express*," he said. "Look. It would be better if you just didn't answer. Cormack's pretty shifty. He's the kind of reporter who can make a mime start talking, and I don't think you're a good enough liar."

"Okay," Sara said, not knowing whether she'd just been complimented or insulted or somehow strangely preempted in her own home. She didn't need protection from her own telephone, for heaven's sake.

When it finally stopped ringing, they both stood there staring at it a moment. Well, actually, Decker was staring bullets at the phone while Sara glared daggers at him.

"Anybody else I'm not supposed to talk to, Lieutenant?" she snapped.

"Nobody," he said. "Not about this, anyway."

Sara rolled her eyes. "You know, yesterday, if I had taken Arbor Avenue instead of Patriot's Parkway, none of this ever would have happened."

"You're right. And if the Ripper hadn't killed seven women, you wouldn't have to worry about becoming the eighth." He stalked to his chair. "Maybe I will have a glass of that wine, after all," he muttered. "You don't have any beer, do you?"

"Yeah," she grumbled. "Heineken, if that's all right with you."

His storm-colored eyes crinkled at the corners, and he laughed. "I like your style, Sara Campbell. And I'm sorry I shouted at you."

"Apology accepted, Lieutenant. I'll be right back with that beer."

Joe brought the long-neck green bottle to his lips and took a small, almost dainty sip, nursing the beer while he waited for Sara to return. After she brought him the beer, she remembered that she hadn't placed her grocery order for the next morning's delivery.

"If I don't get the order in by midnight," she'd said

before she'd gone upstairs, "they add a five-dollar surcharge to their fee."

She was careful about money. He liked that. Even more, he liked the fact that she wasn't the rich candy heiress he'd presumed. Her cash flow problems seemed to make her more accessible, although for what Joe wasn't sure. He was sure, though, that he needed to keep his mind on business, so he set the half-full beer bottle on the coffee table, then headed upstairs to check the windows he should have attended to earlier.

He tested the front door one more time before climbing the wide marble staircase that led to the second floor. The oil paintings that lined the stairwell made him feel more like a museum guard than a homicide detective. My God, it would take a platoon to adequately secure this place and to protect Sara while she was in it. He ought to get her out of here whether she wanted to go or not. Maybe he should arrest her for her own good, he thought, only half in jest.

At the top of the stairs, he glanced left and right, then turned right down the wide hallway toward the spot where a wedge of yellow light cut across the thick carpet. Through the partly open door he saw Sara sitting cross-legged in a large swivel chair, staring intently at a computer monitor, oblivious of everything except whatever was on that screen. He couldn't decide whether to be annoyed that she wasn't taking her predicament more seriously or happy that she seemed to feel safe in his care.

Hell, maybe he was all wrong about the Ripper. Maybe the guy packed up his ski mask and left town once somebody IDed him. Maybe Sara wasn't in danger at all and that phone call was just a wrong number.

Yeah. And maybe it would be eighty-five degrees tomorrow and the sun would come up in the west.

Even though the door was open, he tapped softly.

"Come on in, Lieutenant," she said without taking her eyes from the monitor or her fingers from the keyboard. "Sorry this is taking so long. Everybody in town must be ordering groceries tonight in this bad weather. What kind of sausages do you like, link or patty?"

"Excuse me?"

She glanced over her shoulder at him. "Sausages. You know. Those things that go with eggs at breakfast."

"Oh, you don't have to—"

"Links," she said, cutting him off as she hit a key. "Oh, patties, too. What the hell." She punched another key.

He stood behind her while her fingers scrambled over the keys and she crammed a virtual shopping cart with wonderful food. Exotic stuff. Leeks and scallions and Greek olives. Capers and mangoes and...

"What the hell is Swiss chard?" he asked when she keyed an X beside it, then shivered when she said it was like spinach, only better.

He pictured his refrigerator with its obligatory six-pack, milk that was sour more often than not and yogurt that always expired before he got in the mood to eat it. Since Edie died, his diet had consisted mainly of fast food and slow antacids.

"There," Sara said. "All done."

The monitor went dark. The only remaining light in the room came from the lamp on the nightstand beside the bed. A big bed, Joe noticed, covered by a fat floral comforter and mounded with at least a score of pillows in every imaginable shape and size, hardly leaving

room for one person, much less two. *Two?* The thought
sort of ricocheted in his brain for a second, taking him
by such surprise that he sucked in a sudden breath, one
that was laden with Sara Campbell's come-hither perfume. He dragged his gaze from the bed to her. Back
to business.

"Okay with you if I just wander around up here,
checking windows?" he asked.

"Sure," she said, unwinding her legs and standing
up. "There are seven bedrooms, though. Maybe I'd
better give you the fifty-cent tour."

"Great." He followed her into the hallway, averting
his eyes from the sway of her backside while he ignored her musky fragrance, less than eager just then to
be visiting six more bedrooms and viewing God knows
how many more seductive beds.

"Last but not least," she said, opening the door and
flipping on the wall switch in her parents' room. Several black-shaded brass lamps lit up to cast a restrained
amber glow on the paneled walls and coved ceiling.
As always, Sara felt as if she were walking into a page
of *Architectural Digest* where everything was slick and
fastidious and perfectly proportioned. Picture perfect.
Just like the couple who had inhabited this room.

"There's a set of French doors behind that Chinese
screen, Lieutenant," she said, pointing to the wall opposite the enormous four-poster bed. "They open onto
a little terrace on top of the music room."

"More doors," he muttered as he headed in that
direction.

Sara remained where she was, mere inches across
the threshold, feeling unwelcome, rather like an intruder, even though her parents had been dead for

eleven months. They'd moved to this house when she was seven, and in the ensuing twenty-four years she probably hadn't spent more than twenty-four minutes in this sanctum sanctorum, as she'd referred to it in her snide teenage days.

A photograph of the couple—dashing Jack and glorious Gloria—smiled at her from an ornate silver frame. There was no room for Sara in the picture, just as there hadn't been much room for her in their lives.

"It's cold in here," she said, hugging her arms around herself, aware that the chill she felt was more than a draft from the open French doors.

She heard Decker pull them closed, heard him mutter a little string of curses as he slid the brass bolts into place. He reappeared, scowling, from behind the tall screen.

"You've got more doors than bloody Buckingham Palace, Sara Campbell."

She laughed. "You're probably right. And I don't need a single one of them, do I? I mean, since I'm not going to be going anywhere."

"I wish you would. Just for a while. Just until…"

"Read my lips, Lieutenant." With her arms still tightly crossed, she fashioned a firm, albeit silent, no.

A growl rumbled deep in his throat, then he stalked toward the bank of windows on the south side of the room, wrestling aside drape after heavy drape to test the locks.

"I doubt that anybody's going to come through a second-story window," she said. "Aren't you taking this a bit too far?"

He wrenched the last set of drapes into place, shooting her a hard glare over his shoulder. "Ever heard of ladders?"

"That would be going to an awful lot of trouble, wouldn't it, for somebody who doesn't even remember what that guy looked like?"

He turned toward her, brushing dust from his hands and sleeves. "Well, hey, what do I know? If I were the Ripper and somebody had pulled off my mask, I guess I'd just assume she'd get some kind of impression of my face. Any normal person would."

"I'm *normal,* Decker," she retorted.

"I didn't mean you, for Christ's sake. I meant *him.*"

"Oh."

He crossed the room in a few long strides until he was standing practically toe to toe with her. "And you're about as normal as a fruitcake at Christmas, Miss Campbell," he said, glaring directly into her eyes.

"Thank you very much," Sara snarled, intending to insult him up one side and down the other before the oddest thing happened and her mouth snapped shut. For all his steely-eyed, nostril-flaring, fire-breathing anger, Joe Decker looked like he wanted to kiss her. And right that moment, mad as she was, Sara wanted him to do just that. Kiss her.

*You are crazy!* she said to herself, before almost yelling at Decker, "Are we through in here?"

"You better believe it." He brushed past her, gnashing his teeth on his way out.

He jabbed the iron poker into the fire as if he were trying to kill it rather than just stoke up the dying coals. He'd been muttering to himself ever since Sara had slammed her bedroom door fifteen minutes earlier. He was a cop and she was a citizen under his protection and he'd just called her a fruitcake, for God's sake.

Plenty of guys had reprimands lodged in their files for less.

A fruitcake! What was worse, though, was that he'd wanted to wrap his arms around the fruitcake and kiss her like she'd never been kissed before, and that was so far out of line that it could earn him a suspension without pay if not a well-deserved dismissal. He took a last stab at the glowing embers.

"I'm sorry I was so touchy, Lieutenant."

When her voice sounded from the doorway, Joe dropped the poker with a harsh clang onto the hearth. Before she was halfway through her sentence, his hand was halfway to his gun. Then he gave a small sigh of relief, and instead of bellowing, *Jesus! Don't sneak up on people like that,* he said, "That's okay. I'm sorry I called you a fruitcake. I was way out of line."

She had changed into something long and black and velvety, and her bare feet didn't make a sound as she walked to the couch. She had replenished her wineglass, Joe noticed.

"I guess I'm not all that normal," she said, settling onto the couch. "But it's not as if I chose to be this way. Agoraphobic, I mean. It just happened."

He levered up from his squat before the fire and moved to the chair, picking up his warm beer in the process. "How?"

"How?" His question seemed to take her by surprise. "How did it happen?" She shook her head a little sadly, pondered the crimson depths of her glass a moment before looking at him. "Thanks, anyway. You really don't want to know."

"I wouldn't have asked if I didn't. Yesterday, when I told my partner, Maggie, about you, she said she had an aunt who hadn't been out of the house in something like a dozen years.''

"That's sad.'' Her sincerity registered on her face as well as in her voice.

"So, how long do you intend to keep yourself cooped up?'' he asked, watching her intently. "A year? Two? Twelve?''

She averted her eyes from his for a moment, which told Joe that she hadn't really thought it out or measured her future in any way. Sara appeared to be living, or not living, as the case might be, directly in the present. And that made sense, he thought. People panicked in the here and now, not next year or twelve years down the road.

"As long as it takes,'' she said softly. A tiny smile, a sad one, twisted the corners of her mouth. "You remind me of my shrink, Decker. Yesterday, when I told him I wasn't coming back, he said I was making a mistake.''

"Maybe. Only you know what's right for you.''

She arched an eyebrow. "So, do you have a degree in psychology, too?''

"Me?'' He chuckled. "Hardly. I flunked the hostage negotiator course two times.''

"Why?''

"Too impatient. The last time I negotiated with a bullet instead of a bullhorn. My supervisors thought I missed the point.''

She laughed, and he was glad to see her worried features smooth out. What a waste, he thought. A woman as beautiful as she was, hiding herself away from all the eyes that would eagerly appreciate her the way his were doing now, skimming from her soft red hair along lush curves of black velvet all the way to her pink toenails. A hell of a waste.

The front doorbell echoed down the long hallway. His gaze flicked to her face. "Were you expecting anybody?"

"No. Nobody. It's nearly ten, isn't it?"

He glanced at his watch as he got up. "Five after. Stay here. I'll see who it is."

The bell rang once more before Joe got there. When he called, "Who is it?" the answer was a stone cold silence that had him reaching for his gun before he wrenched open the door on the very last face he had expected to see. His captain. Frank Cobble.

From the sudden flare in the captain's eyes and the quick compression of his lips, it was obvious that he hadn't expected to see Joe, either, and from his harsh tone of voice it was obvious that he wasn't one bit pleased.

"What are you doing here, Decker?"

"Just hanging out, Captain." Joe eased his revolver, unnecessary, into its holster, then he grinned, all innocence, knowing the display would rub his supervisor's notorious ulcer like sandpaper.

"I told you there's nothing in the budget for overtime on this." Cobble's words came out like hissing steam in the cold night air.

"I'm on my own clock, Frank. What about you? You're usually tucked into your bed by this time every night, aren't you?"

"For your information, Decker, I've been known to work past five a time or two. Especially now, with the press all over our asses about this Ripper."

Especially now that they had a witness, Joe thought,

and nine-to-five Cobble could grab a little last-minute glory with very little effort.

"How's our witness?" the captain asked, confirming Joe's suspicions. "I thought I'd just check on her, you know, to make sure she's all right. I drive right by here on my way home every night, anyway, so I thought I'd stop."

"She's asleep," he answered tersely.

"You brought her in to look at the mug shots today?"

"She looked at them, but she couldn't ID anybody. Maybe her head will be clearer in a day or two."

The captain was silent for a moment, no doubt disappointed that he wasn't going to be giving a press conference the next day or seeing his picture in the paper. Then he turned up the collar of his perfectly pressed and neatly belted trench coat and stepped back from the door. "You let me know the minute she comes up with anything, all right? Anything. You call me at home if you have to."

"Will do, boss." Joe sketched a little Boy Scout cross over his heart just to irritate him.

"See you later, Decker," he snarled before turning down the walk.

When Joe called out, "Watch your step, Frank. It's slippery out there," the only response he got was a quick brush of the man's leather-gloved hand.

He closed the door and locked it. Sara Campbell owed him one, he thought. He'd just spared her an interrogation that would have been about as subtle and unpleasant as a beating with a rubber hose.

She was curled up on the couch when he returned to the den, her empty wineglass about to tumble from her lax hand. When he removed it as gently as possible, her eyes blinked open.

"I must have fallen asleep," she said. "Who was at the door?"

"My boss."

Her forehead creased and she struggled to sit up. "You're not in trouble for bringing me those pictures, are you?"

"Nah. He was just checking on his star witness." When he watched her stifle a yawn, he said, "Why don't you go on up to bed? I'll just hang out down here."

"Maybe I will."

He reached out his hand to help her up. The wine had made her wobbly, and when she leaned against him, Joe breathed in the musky scent of her perfume and felt the womanly warmth of her beneath the sleek black velvet and wanted her with an intensity he hadn't felt in years.

"Sorry," she said, steadying herself with a hand on his arm. Her touch, light as it was, flared through him like a Roman candle. He felt his jaw tighten and his expression flatten in his effort to tamp down on the sudden, serious lust.

"Well, good night," he said, stepping back and snatching a magazine from the coffee table, opening it and beginning to read even as he sat.

"You're welcome to sleep in any of those other bedrooms upstairs, Lieutenant."

He glanced from the page—"This is fine, thanks"— then back to whatever gibberish was printed there, aching for her to leave so he could begin to cool off.

"All right, then," she said, yawning again on her way out the door. "See you in the morning."

"Right." Morning. When he would have to batten down his lust all over again. He was really looking forward to that.

# Chapter 5

The next morning Sara's grocery order arrived at seven-thirty, much earlier than she'd expected considering the amount of snow that had come down, a goodly portion of which was on her kitchen floor after Kelvin brought in the last ice chest from his truck. The husky delivery man looked more like a longshoreman this morning in his knit cap and navy pea coat.

"It's bad out there," he said, while he emptied the contents of the ice chest onto the island.

"I appreciate your getting here so early, Kelvin."

"Oh, that's okay. When I shopped out your order, it looked like you had a bunch of breakfast stuff, so I put you first on my list. No mangoes today, though. Sorry about that."

"No big deal," she said, relieved that he hadn't decided to substitute some khaki-colored, unrecognizable fruit that she'd only wind up throwing away. Kelvin had been shopping her orders for long enough now that he was beginning to second-guess her, often with disastrous results.

He was a sweetheart, though, and oddly gentle for someone with hands like slabs of baby back ribs and a neck as big around as Sara's thigh. Since her panic attacks had worsened, sometimes Kelvin was the only human being she would see in the space of a week. Well, Kelvin and Dr. Bourne. Now there was no more Dr. Bourne.

"How's your mom's rheumatism, Kelvin?"

"She's achy," he said. "This snow's no help. Or the cold. Hey, you want me to put some of this in the freezer for you?"

"I can get it," she said. "Thanks, anyway. I'll just sign for it so you can get on your way."

"Okeydoke." He fumbled through some papers until he located her order, then vainly searched behind his ears and in the pockets of his pea coat for a pen.

"Never mind," Sara said. "There's a pen over here in the drawer."

When she turned to get it, though, she slipped in a little puddle of melted snow. Her feet started going out from under her, and her arms began to pinwheel, and all she could think was that she was going to crack her head again and, if she lived, she'd have to be rushed to that horrible hospital. Given a choice, she thought, she'd really rather die.

Then Kelvin caught her, and she was safe, even if momentarily smothered in wet navy wool and the mingled odors of produce and perspiration.

"Hold it right there," Lieutenant Decker's voice resounded from the doorway.

"No!" Sara screeched, untangling herself from Kelvin's arms, then standing protectively in front of him.

"This is my delivery man, for heaven's sake. I lost my balance and he caught me."

The lieutenant rolled his eyes, lowered his revolver and let out his breath in a curse. Kelvin, meanwhile, stood as frozen as a snowman, his mouth agape and his eyes like huge black coals.

"Kelvin, it's all right," Sara said. "It's okay. This man is just—"

"Her brother," Decker said, cutting her off as he reholstered his weapon.

Sara blinked. "My...?"

The lieutenant fashioned one of his ravishing grins, aimed it at Kelvin and said, "I'm a little overprotective. Sorry."

Kelvin started to breathe again. Well, pant, actually, Sara noticed, while he hurriedly gathered his empty canvas sacks and his ice chest and order forms.

"Let me find a pen and I'll sign that for you," Sara offered, but poor Kelvin was already halfway out the door.

"S'okay, Miss Campbell," he called over his shoulder. "Really. S'okay. We'll take care of that next week. Bye."

Sara whirled to the man who was leaning a shoulder against the door frame, still grinning that killer grin.

"My brother!" she exclaimed. "My *brother?*"

He added a shrug to the grin. "I didn't think he'd buy it if I said I was your sister."

The man made it impossible for her to laugh and be irritated at the same time, so Sara laughed. "Why all the mystery?" she asked, picking up an egg carton and a gallon of milk on her way to the refrigerator.

"The fewer people who know about your little run-in with the Ripper, the better. I don't want this to turn into a circus with you as the star attraction.'' He was silent a minute. Then, while Sara rearranged the contents of her refrigerator to make room for the new groceries, she heard the lieutenant mumbling.

"Onions. Green pepper. Hmm. Mushrooms.'' His mumble clarified into his usual sexy baritone. "You know, I used to make a really mean omelette. Bring those eggs back over here.''

Joe was doing fine with his one-handed egg cracking—a quick shot on the rim of the bowl, a controlled drop followed by a perfect lob of empty shell into the garbage disposer—until the sixth egg, which cracked, seemingly all by itself, and ran down the outside of the bowl to form a yellow, viscous pool on the white-tiled countertop. "God bless it!" he swore.

"The paper towels are just to your right,'' Sara said from her post at the stove where she was tending the sausages. "As we say in the antique business, Decker, 'You break it, you bought it.'''

He sopped up the egg, then broke another one—two hands this time—and began whisking them with a fork. Whatever had possessed him to cook an omelette, Joe had no idea. One minute he was drawing his service revolver on a guy in Sara's kitchen; the next minute he was wearing an apron, crying from chopping onions and beating the hell out of half a dozen eggs. Well, he was hungry, he reassured himself, and he didn't want Sara to sneak anything weird into his breakfast, like Swiss chard or capers.

When the omelette was done, however, she managed to sneak something onto his plate, after all. Something that looked like a small circle of green gelatin with little black bugs in it. And after she informed him it was kiwifruit, he was even more determined not to eat something that smacked of shoe polish and extinct birds.

"For somebody so fearless with criminals and delivery people, Lieutenant, you're a real weenie when it comes to food," Sara said. "Didn't your mother make you eat everything on your plate?"

"Yeah, she did. Every last piece of meat and potatoes," he said. "And for somebody who's such a weenie in general, Miss Campbell, eating kiwi isn't going to exactly get your picture on the cover of *National Geographic*."

"I am *not* a weenie." She put down her fork, glaring across the table at him. Her eyes were greener by far than the disputed fruit. "Well, not here, anyway. Not when I'm home."

They had brought their plates into the sunny breakfast room off the kitchen. Ivy climbed the wallpaper and curtains. It twined around the legs of the glass-top table through which Joe had been eyeing Sara's slim legs and slender feet while he ate. She'd traded yesterday's jeans for black leggings along with a bulky white sweater that tried but failed to hide her generous curves. He caught himself thinking again what a waste it was for her to reside permanently behind locked doors.

"I'll make a deal with you," he said. "I'll eat my kiwifruit if you'll go out to dinner with me. Maybe catch a movie."

"You're asking me out?"

"Well, yeah." He hadn't meant to. It had just slipped out, taking him as much by surprise as it had her. "Dinner and a movie. Nothing threatening about that."

"Not for you," she said. "For me it's comparable to going over Niagara Falls in a barrel. We can have dinner and a movie right here."

"What? Swiss chard and *Sleeping Beauty?*"

She picked up her plate, then shot from her chair. "That's not funny, Lieutenant. Don't you have to go back to work or something?"

"I am at work."

When she rounded the table on her way to the kitchen, Joe caught her arm, holding it when she tried to pull away. "You can't stay here all your life, Sara," he said softly.

"Wanna bet?" She jerked her arm out of his grasp and disappeared through the kitchen door, leaving Joe sitting there, staring at cold eggs and a green circle of fruit that was beginning to look like one big smirking eye.

He hadn't asked a woman out in three years, then he'd done it almost by accident. With a damned nutcase, no less. And she'd turned him down. It probably was time for him to get back to work, or something.

He was chopping the ice off the windshield of his Mustang when Maggie wheeled the big Crown Victoria into the drive. One look at her face, and he could tell that her date with the security guy at Saint Cat's had been a bust. His own face, he thought, probably looked the same. Like he'd been sucking lemons.

"How was last night?" he called out.

"Don't even ask." She plowed through the foot of snow to stand beside him. "How'd it go here?"

"One suspicious phone call and one late-night inspection by nine-to-five Frank," he said, delivering a blow with the scraper that freed one wiper.

"You're kidding? Cobble was here?"

"Yeah, but he's not going to be giving any press conferences today." He reached across the windshield to attack the other frozen blade.

"So she didn't ID any of the pictures, huh?"

"Nothing."

Maggie sighed, and her breath wreathed around her head a moment in the cold air. "Well, you go ahead and take off. I'll stay with her today."

Those were the exact words Joe thought he wanted to hear, but as soon as his partner spoke them, he felt a little thread pull tight in his chest. "That's okay." He avoided Maggie's eyes by concentrating on the icy glass. "I'll stay."

He could feel her eyes on him, two blue lasers boring through the back of his head. Maggie knew him better than he liked to admit. When nobody wanted to work with him after the First Federal Savings and Loan episode last year—when he'd ignored the hostage negotiators out front and broken in a back window, then handcuffed the asshole robber while he was screaming into the phone—it was Maggie who'd stood up and volunteered. Her first words to him in the squad car were, "Listen, Sue. I like my life, okay? So I'd appreciate it if you'd leave your death wish at home."

And he had. Pretty much.

"Do you think this is a good idea, Joe?" Maggie asked him quietly.

"Probably not, Mag," he said. "But I'm staying, anyway. I've already called in sick."

He gave her the pay phone number he'd scribbled the night before, asking her to check it out and get back to him. Then, as she was backing out of the drive, "Oh, and tell Cobble that no news is just that. No news."

* * *

Sara stared at the monitor of her computer. It might just as well have been blank for all its images of plates and teacups and saucers registered on her brain. Lieutenant Decker had asked her out. Her heart had done a happy, surprised little tap dance, and she'd yearned to say yes, but instead she'd said no way. *Out* was something she just didn't do anymore.

The thing was, she thought, when she'd told Dr. Bourne she was going home to stay, she hadn't intended to meet anybody who'd tempt her to leave. She hadn't foreseen dinner with Joe Decker across a candlelit table or a movie with his arm brushing hers in a dark theater. Dammit. Enticing as those thoughts were, they were closing her throat and tightening her chest.

She wished she'd never met him. Or that he were different. Not a muscled, fearless, gun-toting, card-carrying adventurer, but somebody who'd be content to burrow away with her here. Somebody who fixed a mean omelette then didn't want to leave. Or worse, try to take her with him when he did.

It wasn't going to work, she told herself, and the sooner she accepted that fact, the better off she'd be. She wished they'd catch the South Side Ripper this afternoon so her life could get back to normal. Well, her version of it, anyway.

Seeking that normalcy, Sara began to make a few changes on her website, marking sold those items that she'd shipped off to buyers last week. Two Fiesta coffeepots. One medium green dessert bowl. A single turquoise tripod candleholder. It had been a good week. She'd cleared over six hundred dollars. This week would probably be even better since two collectors were frantically trying to outbid each other for the red ten-inch vase that had only cost her four bucks. She'd probably clear six or seven hundred on that alone. Not too shabby for a nutcase, she thought.

A soft knock sounded at her door. Sara called, "Come in," then swiveled to see the lieutenant's face, flushed with cold, peek around the edge of the door. "I thought you'd left," she said, trying to disguise the pleasant surprise in her voice. "I assumed your partner was going to baby-sit me now."

"You're stuck with me, I guess."

Or he was stuck with her, Sara thought.

He came up behind her to peer at the monitor. "Those look just like the dishes my mother had when I was a kid," he said.

"Well, if she still has them, they're probably worth a lot of money."

"No kidding?"

She pointed to a pitcher the color of a green Tic-Tac on the left side of the screen. "This little beauty goes from anywhere from eight hundred to a thousand dollars, depending on its condition."

Joe whistled through his teeth. "Jesus. What's it made of? Solid gold?"

"Solid clay," she said. "Just pottery. It's called Fiesta."

"So this is what you do? Buy and sell this stuff."

She nodded. "I'd make your mother a nice offer for hers if she was interested."

"I'll ask her when I see her next week. She and my dad are planning a big bash for their fortieth anniversary. In the meantime, though, could I interest you in my used set of paper plates? I'd even throw in a service for eight of plastic forks and spoons."

Sara looked over her shoulder. "Don't you have

anything from when you were married? Wedding gifts? Silver and china?"

He shook his head. "Too many memories. I hauled it all to Goodwill." He gave a little chuckle. "Some bum's probably eating pork and beans off our Royal Copenhagen right this minute."

There was so much muted sadness in his smile and such pain in his eyes that it made Sara's heart ache. "How long were you married?" she asked. "Or would you rather not talk about it?"

"No. It's okay. Ten years. Or almost. Edie died just a few days before our tenth anniversary."

"What happened?"

"She was crossing Lymond Boulevard just as a drunk made a wide right turn against a red light."

Sara flinched. "Oh, God."

"She never knew what hit her," he said with a kind of grim finality. "Listen, I don't want to keep you from your work. I just came up to ask where I can take a shower since there's no tub in that bathroom off the kitchen."

"Oh. I didn't even think about that. I'm not used to having guests. Er, I mean…"

"Baby-sitters," he corrected her.

"I've pretty much cleaned out all the bathrooms," she said. "You might as well go ahead and use mine." She pointed across the room where a door stood ajar. "Right there."

"Okay." He started toward it.

"There are fresh towels in the closet."

"Okay."

"Oh. And Decker?"

He turned back. "Yeah?"

"I know you're a detective, but don't snoop, okay?"

* * *

What the hell did she think he'd snoop for, anyway? Joe wondered while he toweled off after his shower. His gaze strayed across the white marble top of the vanity. He identified the perfume that was driving him crazy. Even the bottle had a sensuous, curvy shape. Other than that, all he saw was the usual, not-so-sensuous assortment of tissues, soap dish, comb and brush and vitamins.

No toothpaste, though. He'd brought his toothbrush yesterday, but forgotten to toss the mangled tube of Crest into his gym bag, so he opened the top right drawer of the vanity where he assumed Sara's would be. It was, along with cotton squares, Band-Aids, disposable razors and—hello!—three, no four, little foil-wrapped, prelubed, extra thin ribbed, for God's sake, condoms.

Joe closed the drawer, then realized he'd left the toothpaste inside, so he opened it again and then stared at the small dark blue packages. It hadn't occurred to him that there might be a man in her life. He'd simply assumed that there wasn't. She hadn't asked for anyone to be notified when she was at Saint Cat's. She hadn't made any quick, reassuring phone calls once she'd gotten home. At least he didn't think so. And she certainly hadn't mentioned anybody. A boyfriend. A lover. A fiancé.

He squeezed out a half inch of toothpaste, stared at himself in the mirror while he brushed and felt like a world-class jerk. *What did you think, Decker? That she was a thirty-year-old virgin? That she was Sleeping Beauty just snoozing until you came along? That there was a place for you in her cozy little cave of a life? Jerk!*

He spat the foam he'd worked up into the sink, then

turned the water on full blast to wash it away. The guy was probably out of town and that's why she hadn't called him. Hell, maybe she had. Maybe she'd lain in that pillow-littered bed of hers for hours last night, whispering to him on the phone. Or sat up half the night composing long and lovelorn e-mail to him. Who knew? Who cared?

All Joe knew, though, was that whoever this guy was, he hadn't taken very good care of Sara, allowing her fears and anxieties to accumulate until they threatened to wall her in. That never would have happened, he thought, if she'd been his. Not in a million years.

He stabbed his legs into a fresh pair of jeans, then gave his clean flannel shirt a couple whacks to get the wrinkles out. He threaded his belt, buckled it, glowered at that top right drawer one last time, then headed downstairs where he'd left his shoes and his gun in the bathroom off the kitchen.

The marble was chilly beneath his bare feet, but Joe went down the staircase slowly, studying the paintings more closely than he had the night before. Damned if there wasn't a Matisse, a circle of dancing leaf shapes on a vivid blue background, right in the middle of the stairs, and, at the bottom, a Picasso. Sara couldn't be too strapped financially if she owned these, he decided. Of course, she couldn't pay the mortgage with a Picasso or a Matisse, and maybe she couldn't bear to part with them.

He, on the other hand, had parted with nearly everything after Edie died, selling the house with most of its contents, then moving the few things he'd kept to a one-bedroom apartment not too far from the precinct house. He'd hardly spent any money these past three years, other than on the bare necessities, so his bank account was pretty flush as a result. There was probably even enough to put a hefty down payment on a Victorian fixer-upper similar to the one he and Edie had had.

He stopped halfway down the long hallway. Why he was thinking about another house he hadn't the vaguest idea. Crazy, he thought. Worse than crazy. Maybe some of Sara's neuroses were rubbing off on him. Probably it was because he hadn't spent any length of time with a woman other than Maggie in the last three years, and half the time he didn't even notice that Mag was a woman. These domestic moments with Sara were just making him a little nostalgic, that was all, uncovering a side of him he'd buried pretty deep. Joe shook his head. A down payment on another big, paint-sucking, time-taking, money-eating Victorian. That'll be the day.

He turned into the kitchen and stopped dead once more. The back door was wide open. "Sara," he called, and when he got no answer he called louder. "Sara!"

Every nerve in his body snapped to life. His gun was in the bathroom to the left. There wasn't time to get it. There was only time to sprint across the kitchen and out the door.

Sara had managed to drag the fifty-pound bag of birdseed from the back door, where Kelvin had left it, all the way across the patio and down the back lawn to the little white-frame structure that once was her playhouse but now served as a utility shack and potting shed.

If she'd had any sense, she'd have waited until Lieutenant Decker finished his shower, then asked him to use those glorious muscles of his to do it for her, but she'd decided that wasn't quite kosher, considering the taxpayers' money that paid his salary. Instead, she'd put on her old thick parka and the ski mask she kept stuck in its pocket and proceeded to wrench nearly every muscle in her body pushing, pulling and pummeling the sack through the foot-deep snow. The birds better appreciate this, she thought.

She stood up as much as she could in the dim, low-ceilinged shack, thinking she should probably push the seed sack in farther, but then deciding the hell with it. Once she locked up, no squirrels would be bothering it unless they had a key. Standing all scrunched over, she twisted her neck right, then left to relieve some of the stress on her spine, then winced and slowly began to back out of the diminutive door.

Something slammed into her with such force that there wasn't even enough time to scream before her body thudded sideways onto the snow-packed ground. Sara heard her breath leave her body with distinct *oof* as a terrible weight pressed her into the cold snow.

She couldn't breathe. Oh, God. She couldn't even move. Everything went pitch black for a second, and then everything went a blinding white when her ski mask was viciously ripped from her head.

A litany of curses cracked in the cold air above her. Sara forced her eyes to focus. If she'd failed to see the Ripper before, this time she intended to succeed, even if it meant that the fiend's face was the last thing she would ever see. What she saw, though, wasn't the Ripper at all, but Joe Decker's livid face. Relief welled up. Then pure rage.

The lieutenant was sitting on her, straddling her rib cage, glowering and peppering her with words like idiot and fool and what the hell was he supposed to think when he saw the drag marks through the snow.

"Get. Off. Me." Her arms were pinned so she couldn't push him. "Now."

He eased one leg to the side, snarling while he shifted his weight. Then, instead of getting up, he knelt beside her and grabbed two fistfuls of her parka to lug her upright. "Are you okay?"

"Barely," she snapped. Her breath had come back, accompanied by a severe case of the shakes.

"What the hell were you doing out here?"

"Bir-birdseed."

"Birdseed," he echoed.

"P-putting it in the shed." She pointed a shaky hand toward the open door. "Would you clo-close the door and lock the padlock, please?"

After raking her with a final glare, he got up and stalked to the shed where he cursed the bag of birdseed, pushing it in farther inside before he slammed the little door closed, then snapped the lock. It was only then that Sara noticed the lieutenant was barefoot and wearing only jeans and a flannel shirt in this bitter cold.

"You're going to freeze to death," she said.

"No kidding." He stomped to her through the snow, then held out a hand to help her up. "Come on. Let's get back inside before we both freeze to death."

Sara was shaking so badly, from the cold and from the aftereffects of the attack, that she couldn't move. Her teeth were chattering, and her bones felt like taffy. "I don't think I can."

Without a word, he bent over and gathered her in his arms, then stood and started for the house. In her down-stuffed parka, Sara kept slipping in his grasp. "This is like carrying the Michelin Man," he grumbled, not breaking his stride as he shifted her against his chest.

"Well, it's your fault," Sara said, not all that irritably, as she clung to his neck, enjoying the sensuous scratch of his jawline against her cheek and the fragrance of her coconut milk shampoo in his damp hair. "You shouldn't have come out like this, Decker. Barefoot and with your head all wet."

"I didn't have much choice."

"What in the world were you thinking?"

"Oh, not much." He jounced her again. "The back door was wide open in twenty-degree weather. There were drag marks across the yard. Being the good detective that I am, I just naturally assumed you were doing something weird with a fifty-pound bag of birdseed." The rough anger was gone from his voice, replaced by a touch of amusement.

"I'm sorry I alarmed you. I never once thought...."

"It's all right."

She was quiet a moment. "I guess I should thank you for blindsiding me."

"You're welcome."

"Did you really think I was the South Side Ripper?" she asked.

"No," he answered, crooking his neck to look at her, beginning to work up that razzle-dazzle thing his mouth did. "I knew it was you all along, Sara Campbell. I just wanted to take your breath away."

And he did just then. He really did.

Jerk, Joe said to himself while he held a long fireplace match to a pile of kindling. Not only had he almost broken every bone in Sara's body, but then, after he'd carried that trembling body to the house, he held her so long that she finally felt forced to clear her throat and suggest it was okay to put her down.

She was upstairs, taking a warm bath to rid herself of the shakes. What she hadn't noticed was that he was shaking, too, not half as much from the cold as from seeing that damn ski mask. In the same moment he'd lunged for the Ripper, he pictured Sara's lovely body, lying in that little shed, bleeding from the deep slashes of that bastard's blade. There wasn't a doubt in his mind that, if it had been the guy, Joe would have killed him right there. No handcuffs. No Miranda. No arrest, except the lethal arrest of his worthless life.

Never before had he lost his head on the job. His temper, sure. He lost that ten or twelve times a day. But he'd never lost his cool. He'd never crossed the line from professional force to private fury. Not until today. He knew that he would have when Edie was run down, but the drunk had been apprehended and booked while he was at the hospital, then stashed safely behind bars until his trial, so Joe had never had a chance to rip him apart the way he wanted to.

The kindling caught, sending gold fingers of flame over the stack of logs, warming his face and reminding him of the heat he'd felt when he'd held Sara in his arms. He'd been as oblivious of the snow under his bare feet as a swami walking over red-hot coals. He'd meant what he said about wanting to take her breath away, but he was relieved that she had laughed at the ridiculously romantic remark. He was, he decided, officially crazier than Sara. But her craziness didn't matter because she was a civilian. His craziness, on the other hand, could get her dead.

He walked to the rolltop desk and punched in a call to Maggie. Just as he suspected, the pay phone had been wiped clean of prints. There was more bad news when she informed him that the department's shrink was on vacation, and Cobble wouldn't authorize a replacement, so there was no way they could use hypnosis to try to prod Sara's memory. The worst news, though, was that Maggie had made plans for the evening after Joe had told her he was staying with Sara.

"Call Underwood," Maggie suggested. "The way he loves women and money, he'd volunteer to baby-sit in a hot minute."

That was the problem, Joe thought after he hung up and returned to the fire. As much as he knew he had to distance himself from Sara Campbell, he wasn't anxious to let anybody else share her sanctuary.

The fire was popping and burning bright by the time Sara came down from her bath half an hour later, looking calm again and none the worse for being tackled by a hundred and eighty pounds of hell-bent cop.

"Feeling better?" Joe asked.

"Much."

She was rubbing her damp hair with a towel. Her face was flushed from the warm bathwater. Her fragrance was already filling the room. The temperature seemed to go up several degrees. Then it plummeted when she informed him coolly, "I'm going back up to my computer to get some work done, Lieutenant. Just make yourself at home. There's sandwich stuff in the kitchen if you get hungry."

"Okay. Thanks."

It was obvious that he'd offended her with that dopey remark about taking her breath away. Hell, he'd offended himself. But he didn't know how to apologize without making it worse, so he didn't say anything.

"Will you be staying here tonight?" she asked.

"It looks that way."

"Okay," she said, sounding neither thrilled nor disgusted. Just cool. Remote. Her breath definitely not taken away, but wholly in her possession. "I'll see you later, then."

Sara was tempted to bang her head against the monitor where the images of pottery had been little more than a multicolored blur for the past few hours. This was no way to run a business, she thought. It was no way to run a *life,* becoming all bumble-brained just because a gorgeous man made a flippant remark. If she had it to do all over again, she would have laughed at him and said, "Yeah. I'll bet you say that to all the girls, Decker."

He probably did, too. Nobody who looked that good suffered from lack of female companionship, Sara was sure. And even if he were on the prowl, a confirmed recluse would be the absolute last choice for a man as vital as he was. Even Carter, who wasn't half as vital as the lieutenant, had walked out on her rather than remain cooped up here. For that matter, her parents hadn't wanted to spend much time with her before her anxieties got the better of her.

She sighed and closed her eyes. Maybe if she tried harder to remember the South Side Ripper's ugly puss, the police could catch him and then she'd have her old life back. Joe Decker would be gone from her house and her mind. But, hard as she tried, that mind still refused to divulge a face. She could see the ski mask, but there was nothing beneath it. Just nothing. No eyes. No nose. No face at all.

She shut down the computer and went downstairs to see about dinner, avoiding the den and the sight of the lieutenant in all his denim and flannel glory. The kitchen was dark at almost five o'clock, so she flipped the lights on and began to gather ingredients for pasta and a salad.

Where was the Parmesan cheese that Kelvin was supposed to bring her? She couldn't make her luscious tagliatelle verdi con aglio without Parmesan. After looking in every cold nook and cranny in the refrigerator, she slammed the door.

"Aw, nuts."

"What's the matter?"

The lieutenant's voice came from the doorway. Sara turned to see him rubbing his eyes, then combing his fingers through his rumpled hair. She guessed that he had fallen asleep in front of the fire and wished she had peeked in to see that.

"Kelvin didn't bring me the Parmesan I ordered," she said, then muttered, "now what am I going to do?"

"No problem. Where's the nearest store?"

"Cooley's," she said. "At Ninth and Westbury."

"Okay. Cooley's it is. Just let me get my shoes on."

Only then did Sara notice that he was shoeless. Sleepy-eyed, rumpled and shoeless, with socks that had holes in both big toes. When he turned to leave, she saw the threadbare heels, and her heart shifted a bit in her chest. Poor Decker. He needed somebody to take care of him better than he took care of himself.

While he was retrieving his shoes, Sara decided to make a list. As long as he was going to Cooley's, he might as well pick up another dozen eggs and maybe a nice red Bordeaux. By the time he returned, wearing his leather jacket and jingling his car keys, she had come up with six more necessities.

"Okay. Let's go," he said. "Where's your coat?"

"What?"

"Where's your coat?"

Sara stared at him. "*I'm* not going, Decker."

He stared back. "Well, I'm not leaving you here alone."

"I'll be fine. Cooley's is only a few blocks away. It won't take more than fifteen or twenty minutes."

"I'm not leaving you alone for fifteen or twenty minutes. Now, come on." He jingled the keys again. "Let's go."

"No."

"Fine." He jammed the keys in his pocket and shrugged out of his coat.

"But what about my Parmesan?"

"Tough."

"Couldn't you just—"

"No," he said, as decisively as she had uttered the word.

Sara stood there fuming, torn between tagliatelle verdi con aglio and plain old spaghetti, stuck between Parmesan and a panic place. Her mouth was already going dry and her palms were getting damp at the thought of standing in the checkout line. A long checkout line. A dozen shoppers, all of them with fistfuls of cents-off coupons, in front of her and behind her. It would be hot in the store, and she wouldn't be able to breathe, but she'd be trapped there with a shopping cart and wouldn't be able to leave when she started getting dizzy and sick.

Maybe, though, just maybe, if she stayed in the warm and cozy confines of the lieutenant's little car. Maybe.

"Oh, all right. Dammit. I'll go with you." She dragged in a deep breath. "But I'm staying in the car,

Decker. I mean it. I'm not setting foot in the store. And that's not negotiable.''

"That'll work," he said casually, as if he hadn't the least idea that Sara had just fought and lost World War Three. "As long as I can keep an eye on you."

Joe tried to make quick work of the ice on the rear window, afraid that Sara would lose her nerve and make a run for the house. She was standing at the edge of the driveway, bundled up, her hands tucked under her armpits, her teeth chattering, looking like she was on her way to the electric chair. He still couldn't believe that she had agreed to go, and it pleased him that she trusted him enough to leave the house. Well, maybe not. Trust probably didn't have anything to do with it. It was just that her need for Parmesan cheese had temporarily outweighed her fears.

He opened the passenger door. "All set?" If she were going to bolt, he thought, this was as good a time as any. But she didn't. After she slid into the seat, he closed the door as quietly as he could before trotting around to the driver's side and sliding into his seat. He twisted the key in the ignition, and as soon as the engine came to life with a deep-throated purr, he put the transmission into Reverse and hit the gas. Too late now, pretty Sara, he thought.

Remembering that she had hummed a golden oldie the day before, Joe turned the radio on and tuned in the local oldies station, catching the Beatles right in the middle of "I Want to Hold Your Hand." He wondered briefly if it would help if he held Sara's hand, then decided against it. She'd probably panic, thinking he was coming on to her, especially after that unfortunate "take your breath away" remark.

It took them all of three minutes to go the three blocks to the little corner market. The heater didn't even have time to warm up before he pulled into the small parking lot. In fact, the car was so cold that Joe really didn't want to leave her in it.

"You sure you don't want to come in with me?" he asked.

"Nope." It was so cold in the car that her answer came out like a puff of smoke.

"Okay. I'll be right back."

"Did I give you the list?" she asked, beginning to rummage through her handbag.

"What list? I thought you just wanted cheese."

"Here."

Joe scanned the piece of paper she gave him. "You sure this is all now?" He grinned. "I mean, as long as I'm in there, I can get eggplant, tofu, more Swiss chard."

"That's not funny, Decker."

"Okay. Lock up after I'm gone. And if you need me, just lay on the horn."

Sara scrunched down in the bucket seat as much to keep warm as to make herself invisible. She could peek over the dashboard into the big front window of the brightly lit store, and every once in a while she could see Joe skimming his shopping cart around the end of an aisle. When he rounded the soup and crackers corner, he came to the window and waved to her. She waved back, sighing out loud, wishing she hadn't added one item after another to the list. They could have had the Parmesan and been home by now if she had used a little restraint.

Rod Stewart started singing "Maggie May" on the

radio. Sara thought a little wistfully about the concert she had gone to ten or twelve years ago, and wondered why she hadn't panicked then in a jostling, shrieking crowd of thousands. The thought of doing that now made her almost nauseated. She turned the radio off and concentrated on the store's window.

Cooley's wasn't all that busy, but when Joe angled his cart into a checkout line there were two people ahead of him. He stood patiently, perusing the display of gum and mints, probably taking in the headlines of the *National Enquirer* and the *Star,* checking out the latest *Cosmo* girl perhaps. Then his eyes snapped toward the customer service booth, and his whole face changed.

Sara sat up and leaned to her left, craning her neck to see whatever it was that Joe had seen, and when she did, her heart rocketed into her throat. There was a man waving a gun in the face of a terrified clerk.

# Chapter 6

When Sara's gaze cut back to Joe, his gun was in his right hand, and with his left he was motioning the customers and clerks to get down on the floor. Then he vaulted over the checkout counter and quickly disappeared from Sara's view.

She sat there, frozen with fear, in addition to the cold, staring wide-eyed while cereal boxes and magazines flew across the store window, a knit cap sailed through the air and red-and-white soup cans rolled crazily across the floor. While the melee was in progress, several men and woman escaped out the front door. They blocked Sara's view momentarily, but when they moved, she saw the robber go sprawling facedown on the floor, immediately followed by the lieutenant, who lodged a knee in the man's back and the muzzle of his gun in his neck. When the subdued robber brought his arms behind him, Joe handcuffed him in one swift, deft movement. Sara imagined the conclusive metal click.

"Thank God," she said, realizing she'd been holding her breath during most of the altercation.

Tires screeched, and flashing lights strobed through the darkness when two black and white squad cars pulled into the parking lot. The uniformed cops raced into the store, preventing Sara from seeing anything but a solid wall of dark blue. But barely a moment later, the blue wall parted as Joe elbowed through. He pushed out the door, holstering his gun as he approached her side of the car. Sara rolled down the window as quickly as she could.

"Are you okay?" he asked, bending to lean his arms on the door.

"Am *I* okay!" There was blood on his face. His knuckles were scraped. There was a rip in the shoulder seam of his jacket. Anger still pulsed in the cords of his neck and pulled hard at the corners of his mouth. "Are *you* okay?"

"Me? Oh, sure. That guy couldn't quite figure out how to juggle a gun and a sack of money and throw a punch at the same time. What an amateur." He grinned. "Let me just go in and sign off on this." His gray eyes searched her face intently. "You sure you're okay?"

Sara nodded, then watched him trot inside the store where he disappeared beyond a sea of blue uniforms. A few minutes later, he was back, unlocking the driver's side door, sliding into the seat and plopping a plastic shopping bag onto her lap.

"I think I got everything," he said. "You might want to check, just in case."

She glanced in the bag. Parmesan. A red Bordeaux. A life-and-death struggle. Hey. No big deal. "Does this always happen when you go to the grocery store, Decker?'' she asked a little breathlessly.

"Not always.'' He started the car, then put his arm on the back of her seat while he maneuvered out of the parking spot and threaded the narrow space between the two squad cars. Before he shifted into Drive, he brushed her cheek with the back of his hand. But it was the look that accompanied his touch that made Sara's heart hold absolutely still.

"You're safe with me, you know," he said softly. "I won't let anything bad happen to you, Sara Campbell. You believe that, don't you?''

"Yes," she whispered. "Yes, I think I do.''

Joe rinsed the thick, soapy lather from his hands under a stream of steaming water that was just bearable until Sara turned the hot water faucet up a few searing degrees.

"Ouch!" He pulled his hands away. "The scrapes aren't all that bad, Campbell. Now it's the second-degree burns that hurt.''

"Don't be such a weenie,'' she said, wrapping a towel around both his hands.

"Sadist,'' he hissed.

While Sara was laughing, Joe managed to maneuver the towel so that he was holding her two hands inside it. He squeezed gently. "Hey. How was it, really? Out in the big, bad world beyond the front door?''

She looked up from the towel and met his gaze. "It was okay. I survived.''

"No pitty pats? No sweaty palms?''

"Just a little. Most of them while you were wrestling with that robber. I was so scared for you I didn't have time to be scared for myself.''

"That's good, Campbell. We're making some progress here." He grinned, fighting the urge to kiss her serious, worried mouth. "Hang around with me long enough and you'll never be scared for yourself again."

"I have the feeling that if I hang around you any longer, Decker, I'll graduate from simple panic attacks to outright terror." She laughed as she pulled her hands from his. "Let's finish this so I can start cooking dinner."

They ate in the den in front of the fire, and the meal was delicious, Joe had to admit, once he got used to the green noodles. Edie, early on, had given up trying to make a gourmet out of a staunch meat-and-potatoes guy. Sara took his grumbling in stride, though, and smiled victoriously when he asked for seconds. He was tempted to ask for thirds because he didn't want the meal to end, and he was afraid to think what might happen next. Or not happen.

She came back from the kitchen with a tray on which she carried a small green coffeepot and two demitasse cups and saucers. Joe recognized it immediately as the Fiestaware he had eaten on when he was growing up.

"Using some of your inventory?" he asked.

She lowered the tray to the coffee table, then sat on the floor beside him. "That's one of the drawbacks of being a collector," she said, lifting the pot and pouring dark espresso into one of the little cups. "Sometimes it's almost impossible to part with certain pieces." When she handed it to him, her hands were shaking just enough to make the cup chatter against its saucer.

Joe gave her a quizzical look, which she proceeded to ignore. She filled her cup, dispensed with its saucer and stared into the fire while she sipped. Beside him again, but somehow far away.

"Was it something I said?" he asked, only half in jest.

"No. It's nothing." She shook her head. "It's silly, really."

"What?"

She sighed. "While I was waiting for the espresso to finish dripping, I started to feel as if I were…as if we were…well, on a date. And then I started getting this ridiculous case of nerves because it's been a long time since I had one. A date, I mean. Which this isn't." She rolled her eyes. "See. I told you it was silly."

He smiled, nowhere near willing to admit to her that he was feeling the same silly way. Only in his case it was sappy. And he was wondering about those little foil packages in her bathroom drawer upstairs. "Well, maybe sometime we could…"

"I know. Dinner and a movie. Thanks, anyway." She took another sip of coffee. "I guess you go out a lot." It wasn't a question, but an assumption, offered in a small, insecure voice.

"Not a lot." He promptly cursed himself for his macho lie. "Never, actually. Hell, I don't know," he said almost gruffly. "I probably forgot how after being married for ten years."

She looked at him, her green eyes reflecting the firelight while the smallest of smiles perched on her lips. "You're a nice man, Joe Decker." She leaned forward and placed a tiny kiss on his cheek. "And now that our non-date is over, I'm going up to sleep. Good night."

"G'night, Sara," he said, not knowing if his voice registered regret or relief or a sappy muddle of both.

*Huge windshield wipers slashed back and forth in front of her while people shrieked and moaned behind.*

*Her mother and father, walking arm in arm beneath a huge umbrella, crossed the street in front of her, never once glancing in Sara's direction. They didn't hear her when she called out to them, so she decided to run after them, only she couldn't get her car door open. The handle had disappeared. All she could find was a series of buttons that didn't do anything, no matter how hard she pressed them.*

*Then, after she had given up, the door opened on its own. The only problem then was that it was a long way down to the pavement, maybe six or seven feet.*

*"What difference does it make?" she told herself. "Jump. It's just a dream."*

*She jumped. It was more than seven feet, though. Closer to seven miles. And while she was falling, the pavement kept retreating beneath her. She was in free-fall, flailing, but then somebody caught her. She laughed, thinking those strong arms belonged to Joe, but when she looked up, it wasn't Joe at all, but the Ripper. His eyes glowed red through the holes of his mask.*

*She had to pull that mask off, but her arms felt heavy as lead, and the harder she tried to lift them, the heavier they became. She tried so hard, again and again. Then, all of a sudden, the Ripper lifted his own gloved hand and tore the mask away himself.*

*Sara saw his face.*

After he heard Sara's cry, Joe was upstairs in a matter of seconds. Racing down the hall, he saw the slice of light at the bottom of her closed bedroom door. He didn't bother to knock.

She was sitting in the middle of her bed, hugging a

pillow to her chest, staring, rocking slightly. He glanced at the windows and then at every corner of the room. Nothing appeared amiss.

"What?" he asked. "What happened?"

"I saw him."

Joe went to the window, tested the lock, then looked at the untrodden snow on the ground below. "You saw the Ripper? Where?"

"In a dream. Well, a nightmare."

He let out his breath in a soft little curse, then put the safety back on his gun and jammed it in the holster. "You scared me to death when you screamed."

"I scared myself to death," she said, hugging the pillow closer. "I saw his face, Joe. The Ripper pulled off his mask and I saw his face. Only…"

"Only what?"

She gave a mournful little sigh. "Only I forgot it as soon as I woke up. I turned the light on and…" She snapped her fingers. "Poof! It was gone." She put the pillow down and sank her fist into it. "Damn."

"Well, a face in a dream isn't all that reliable, anyway." And neither was his talent for guessing what a woman wore to bed, he thought. He'd pegged Sara as a flannel pajama type, but he was looking at a pale pink concoction right out of a Victoria's Secret catalog. He was inordinately grateful when she picked up the pillow and hugged it again.

"Go back to sleep," he said, conscious of the sudden thickness in his voice.

She bit her lower lip and shook her head. "Too scared. What a wimp, huh?"

"I'm here."

"You weren't *here*. You were *there*." She pointed in the general direction of the den downstairs. Then she shivered and rubbed her arms. "God. I don't think I'll ever sleep again."

He didn't like where this was heading. Not one bit. Because he knew when she turned those big green eyes to him and asked him to stay with her, here in her room, he'd say the dumbest, most dangerous thing he'd ever said. *Yes.*

"Joe, would you...?" Her gaze, glistening with tears, flattened him.

"Sure. Till you fall asleep, anyway."

He lifted his arm to consult the glowing face of his watch. Three-fifteen, and counting. Beside him, Sara had been asleep for a long time. He'd actually heard the precise moment when her breathing evened out. He'd almost been able to feel her muscles melt into relaxing sleep way over on her side of the big bed.

Edie used to sleep like a Flying Wallenda, flipping over, flopping around, corkscrewing toward the left until she wound up with all of the sheet and nine-tenths of the blankets. Sara slept like a corpse, on her back with her hands delicately crossed over the neat covers. He'd leaned over once to make sure she was still alive, and her soft, warm, toothpaste-scented breath had reassured him and stirred him all at once.

He shifted a few of the pillows that banked his shoulders and head, checked his watch again, then closed his eyes. It's a job, Decker, he told himself, whether it's horizontal or not. Don't even think about kissing her. Later, maybe, when all this Ripper business was over...

A loud, metallic crash in the vicinity of the garage brought him up fast from his nest of pillows. Sara, the corpse, shot straight up, too.

"What was that?" she whispered.

"Probably just a dog knocking over a trash can." He stood, deciding to wait until he was out of the room to take out his gun. No sense scaring Sara if he didn't have to. "I'll go check. Be right back."

She turned on the lamp beside the bed. "Okay. But, Joe..."

"What?" he asked, halfway in the hall.

"I don't have metal trash cans. They're plastic."

He tried the back door in the kitchen, glad to discover it locked up tight before he turned the dead bolt and stepped outside, muttering an oath when his socks encountered the slushy snow on the back porch. It was punishment, he thought bleakly, for lying down on the job. But at least he didn't have to worry about his shoes crunching in the snow when he moved around the rear of the house toward the garage.

The trash cans were undisturbed with both their plastic covers battened down. Nearby, however, he noticed that the metal drainpipe was crimped about a foot off the ground as if something had crashed into it. And, sure enough, when he scouted around, he found one of those metal flying disks that kids used in the snow and, around it, a scramble of footprints. The backyard had a pretty good slope to it, probably irresistible to teenagers out a lot later than they should have been.

He picked up the disk and sent it sailing toward the evergreens at the back of the yard. He heard it thud. Then a voice—about fifteen, Joe guessed, from the inelegant depth of it—called out, "Thanks, man."

Joe stifled a smile. "No problem, man."

At least it wasn't the problem he had anticipated,

and he was grateful for that. He went inside, turned the dead bolt, then tugged off his soaking wet socks.

Upstairs, Sara wasn't in bed where he'd left her. "Sara?" he called softly.

"I'm in here," came the muffled reply.

"In where?"

"The closet."

"What the hell are you...?" He opened the louvered door. He didn't see her at first, but then he caught a glimpse of frothy pink with pink toenails sticking out. "What are you doing in there?"

"I'm hiding, dammit."

He heard a distinctly wet sniff and suddenly realized she was crying. *Aw, jeez.* "It's okay, babe. It was just a kid taking a joyride on a metal tray. Here." He reached into the closet. "Take my hand. Come on."

"This is stupid," she said, letting him lead her to the bed. "I think it finally really dawned on me that somebody might be trying to kill me."

"Yeah, but he's not going to, is he, with me here?" He turned back the covers on her side of the bed. "Climb in."

She paused. "Would you just hold me for a minute? Please?"

Without another word, Joe gathered her against him. Her arms, trembling, circled his waist, and she held on tight. He tried not to even think about how perfectly she fit, how warm her hair was against his cheek, how her fragrance mesmerized him.

"Better?" he asked.

She nodded against his chest, then sighed softly. "This is probably against regulations, isn't it?"

"Maybe just a little."

A moment later Sara loosened her arms. She took a

small step back, then lifted her face. "I'm fine now. Thank you."

"Well, you know our motto." He needed to kiss that generous mouth of hers right then even more than he needed to breathe. "To serve and protect and administer hugs when necessary."

She smiled, and her moist eyes sparkled. "Then you're very good at your job, Lieutenant."

The job, Decker, he warned himself. "Get some sleep now. I'll be right here beside you." On the damn job.

When Sara woke, the first thing she did was glance at the clock on the nightstand. It was seven-ten. Then she stretched, and her hand encountered hard, flannel-covered muscle. Decker! Good lord, how could she have forgotten?

She turned on her side, quietly, hoping not to wake him, wanting to watch him sleep for some absurd reason. His mouth was softer than when he was awake. The frown lines on his forehead had smoothed out. Now that his eyes were closed, she noticed how long and thick his lashes were. Then one gray eye squinted at her, and his lips tilted in a grin.

"You were awake the whole time! No fair," she said, giving his arm a little punch.

"I'm guarding your body."

The other gray eye opened, and his sleepy gaze strayed over her face for a moment before it centered on her mouth. Sara's stomach did a kind of swan dive while her heart surged with an extra beat. Her breath stalled in her throat. Joe was taking it away again without even touching her.

Her lips parted just a bit, and she willed him to kiss

her. Wanted him to kiss her more than she'd ever
wanted anything in her life. Her eyes drifted closed in
anticipation. Her heart stood still.

And then his pager shrilled.

*Saved by the bell. You almost lost it, idiot.*

Joe reached to the floor and snagged the beeper he'd
left there the night before. It was Maggie, God bless
her. And it wasn't the first time she'd gotten him out
of trouble. It probably wouldn't be the last, either.

Without being asked, Sara handed him the handset
of the phone on her side of the bed. He sat up against
the mountain of pillows and punched in her number
and extension at work. "What's up?"

"What *is* up?" Sara asked him a minute later when
he passed the phone back. "Joe?"

"The guys in the Eighth Precinct brought in a Peeping Tom last night."

"A Peeping Tom!" Sara laughed. "I didn't know
the police used that expression."

"He confessed," Joe said.

"To what? Peeping?" She giggled some more.

"To being the South Side Ripper."

Her laughter faded instantly, and her face took on a
kind of befuddled expression that might have been a
mirror image of his own. He didn't know what she was
thinking, but his brain was doing a good-news-bad-
news number. The good news was the son of a bitch
Ripper was finally behind bars. The bad news was that
playing house with Sara Campbell had just come to an
end.

"Well, that's good news," she said. "If he's really
the one."

"Hell of a thing to confess to if he's not." He
reached for her hand, held it in both of his while he

kept his voice absolutely level. "We need you for a lineup, Sara."

"Oh, no. No way."

She tried to pull away, but Joe tightened his grasp. "You can do it."

"No, I can't. I won't. Anyway, if I can't remember what he looks like, what difference does it make if I look at a lineup or not?"

"Maybe if you saw him, you'd remember."

"Don't make me do this, Joe." Her voice climbed to a higher register. "Please. My heart's already pounding and my hands are starting to sweat."

"I know." He turned her hand palm up, then brought it to his lips, placing a gentle kiss on the moist surface. "I'll be with you. I'll hold your hand the whole way. I won't let anything bad happen to you, Sara."

She stared at their joined hands for a long time, trembling, her lower lip snagged between her teeth. Whatever agony she was suffering, whatever hell she was going through, was obvious even though Joe couldn't begin to understand. He hated himself for putting her through this and tried to think of an alternative to a lineup, knowing there was none. This was one regulation he wasn't going to be able to break for her. He couldn't even bend it.

Her big green eyes sought his. "Couldn't I just…?"

"No," he said firmly.

She stared at the closet as if wishing she could crawl in and close the door the way she had the night before.

"I wish I knew what you were afraid of, babe. Whatever it is, I'll take care of it. Tell me. What are you afraid will happen?"

"It's stupid," she said.

"Tell me anyway." He put his arm around her trembling shoulders, drawing her closer. "Tell me."

"What if I start feeling dizzy? What if I faint?"

"I'll catch you."

She let out an exasperated little sigh. "What if I start feeling sick? What if I throw up?"

"What if you do? People puke at the station all the time. You'd fit right in."

This time she gave a tiny laugh. "I'm serious."

"So am I." He gathered her closer. "Look. Here's what we'll do. I'll make sure we get there just before the lineup so we don't have to wait around. We go in. You look. We come home."

"What about the fainting part?" she asked, only half in jest.

"Okay. We go in. You look. You faint. I catch you. Then we come home. How's that?"

She took in a deep breath. "All right. I'll try. But only if you promise me that if I say take me home, you'll do it. Right then. No questions asked."

"You've got a deal."

"No. Say you promise."

He did, even though he knew—if and when the time came—it wouldn't be a promise he could keep.

# Chapter 7

They were sitting in Joe's car half a block from the precinct house. It was snowing again, and he had the heater turned up so high that Sara had to roll her window down. As always, in one of her panicky states, she was either too hot or too cold. There was never a happy, comfortable medium.

She was practicing the abdominal breathing that Dr. Bourne had suggested while she read license plates on passing traffic, trying to distract herself from all the things going haywire inside her. Poor Decker, she thought. He was trying to be so patient and supportive. He had made call after call that morning, trying to get the lineup scheduled at a specific time rather than the usual approximate one. He warmed up the car before she got in, then drove one-handed in order to keep his right hand free to clasp hers reassuringly. Either that, or he was just being prepared to grab her if she tried to escape.

"It's ten fifty-seven," he said, looking at his watch. "That gives us three minutes to get to the viewing-room window. You'll look through the one-way glass for, oh, five seconds maybe. Three minutes back to the car. At eleven-oh-three, you'll be a free woman."

She slanted him a weak grin.

"You can hold it together for six minutes, babe." Once more, he squeezed her hand. "I know you can."

"Don't be so sure," she said to his back as he got out, then trotted to the curb and began feeding change into the meter. Sara rolled her window down a few more inches. "You better not be putting any more than ten minutes on that contraption, Decker."

"Trust me." He held his hand over the vicinity of his heart for a minute before he pushed one more coin into the slot, then opened Sara's door.

"I really don't want to do this," she said through clenched teeth.

"The sooner you do it, the sooner it'll be over. Come on." He held out his hand to her. "Six minutes. Piece of cake."

A uniformed policeman passed on the sidewalk. "Yo, Sue," he called to the lieutenant. "How's it going?"

"Hey, Smitty," Joe responded, then turned his full attention to Sara.

"What did that man call you? Did he say Sue?"

"Uh-huh." He wiggled his fingers. "Come on."

"Sue?"

"That's my nickname."

"Why in the world would anybody call you Sue, Decker?"

"Well, I'll tell you." He grinned. "*After* the line up."

"That's not fair," she said.

"Maybe not, but it'll give you something to think about besides your heart rate and your blood pressure." He grasped her hand and hauled her up and out, then propelled her along the sidewalk toward the station.

Once they were inside the building, it occurred to Joe that the viewing room was on the third floor near the lockup. He prayed while he hit the up button on the elevator, half-expecting Sara to flip out when the door slid open, blissfully relieved when she responded to the little nudge her gave to the small of her back and stepped inside. That wasn't to say she was fine, though. Far from it. Her face was the color of cooked spaghetti, and just about as expressionless. When the elevator shuddered to a halt on the third floor and the door whooshed open, Sara was out like a jackrabbit.

"Where's this one-way window?" she asked, her eyes unusually bright and her voice high and tight.

"Just a few doors down." He took her hand and started down the corridor, threading between uniformed cops and copying machines. "You're doing fine, babe."

"That's what you think. Let's just get this over with."

Maggie was waiting for them at the window. Joe was surprised the captain wasn't there to cash in on the victory if Sara came up with an ID.

"Where's Cobble?" he asked.

His partner shrugged. "He's supposed to be here, but he hasn't shown up yet. Do you want to wait?"

"No way." He could feel Sara's hand tightening like a vise on his, almost hear her heart bashing against her ribs. "Let's do it."

"I know how hard this is for you, Miss Campbell," Maggie said. "Thanks for coming."

Sara nodded, trying to smile, swallowing hard.

"There are six men in there," Maggie told her. "None of them can see you, so you don't have to worry about that. Take your time, okay?"

"Okay."

Maggie opened the venetian blinds that covered the window of one-way glass. Joe glanced at the six men, then, over Sara's head, shot his partner a questioning look. In response, Maggie subtly held up two fingers. Joe looked back. His first impression was that the guy in the number-two spot wasn't as tall or muscular as the guy he'd chased the other day. Still, he hoped Sara could point him out and put an end to this whole bloody business.

Her hand trembled in his while her eyes scanned the six men. Once. Twice. Then she shook her head.

"No. Nothing. None of them looks at all familiar."

"Look just once more," Maggie said.

She did, and came up with the same result. Nothing. "Can we go now?" she asked Joe. "Please?"

Sara fixed lunch for them when he brought her home after the unsuccessful lineup. She didn't know how she could have done it without her clammy hand in Joe's. The six minutes he had promised her turned out to be twelve, but she had survived, mostly thanks to him.

The lieutenant was unusually quiet during the ride home, and those famous grins of his were few and far between even while he ate his ham on rye. He didn't even question the radicchio on the sandwich or accuse her of trying to poison him with something suspiciously purple. Suddenly she remembered that he hadn't told her about his nickname.

"How's the sandwich, Sue?"

"Oh, that." He rolled his eyes. "I was sort of hoping you'd forget."

"Not on your life. And I'm assuming it isn't short for Suzanne."

He grimaced slightly, then peeled back the bread on his sandwich. "What's this purple stuff?"

"Radicchio. Don't change the subject, Decker."

"Suicide," he mumbled.

"What?"

"Sue is short for suicide."

Sara's eyes widened. "I don't even want to know how you got a nickname like that."

"Good," he said. "End of subject." And it was clear from his expression that he didn't want her to pursue the origin, much less the meaning, of Sue.

"Well, it's pretty much all over now, I guess," Sara said a bit wistfully, feeling guilty that she wasn't happier about the South Side Ripper finally being in custody.

"Pretty much, I guess."

"Thanks for being so kind to me, Joe. I'm sure I wasn't the easiest witness to work with."

"No problem." One corner of his mouth crooked up. "You did fine, Sara. You came through like a real trooper."

She smiled, then tried to sound casual when she said, "I'm going to miss you, Decker. Who's going to boss me around now?" *Who's going to hold me when I'm scared?* she thought. *Or just be here making me feel warm and secure?* How could she have gotten so used to this man in just a few days? She didn't feel like a real trooper. She felt sad, forlorn.

Joe, on the other hand, seemed anxious to get back to work. Real work out in the real world, rather than just hanging around here with her. Sue, Sara suspected, needed those thrills and chills as much as he needed air to breathe. After lunch, he didn't waste any time before he gathered all his things. He wrote down several phone numbers for her—the precinct house, his pager, his home.

"Call anytime if you need me," he said.

*I need you now.* "I'll be fine."

"I know you will." He tipped her chin as if he were going to kiss her, but then merely traced his thumb along her jawline and brushed the backs of his fingers across her cheek.

*What about dinner and a movie? No, don't ask me. You know I can't go. But even so, I wish you'd ask.* "Goodbye, Joe."

"Bye, Sara."

She shut down her computer early that night, unable to concentrate on pottery and prices when her gaze kept straying to the bed where Joe had slept beside her the night before. But he'd been merely doing his job, hadn't he? And now, with the Ripper put away, that job was over, and Sara felt a little bit foolish for having considered it anything else.

That night, when Joe walked into his apartment shortly after ten o'clock, he dreaded turning on the lights. He'd stayed at the precinct house, catching up on paperwork, until his eyes felt like sandpaper each time he blinked, and his chest burned from too much coffee and too many greasy burgers and fries.

"Home, sweet home," he muttered, tossing his gym bag into a corner already crammed with a stack of old newspapers and half a dozen towels he'd been meaning to wash. His pullout bed looked just the way he'd left it Monday morning—one scrunched pillow, one wad of pilly wool blanket, two bedraggled sheets.

Sometimes he had the distinct impression that Edie was gazing down on him, shaking her head, with one of those bemused and beleaguered *Aw, Joey* expressions on her face. Ordinarily, when that happened, his throat would constrict and then he'd grumble, "I'm doing the best I can, sweetheart." But tonight he knew that wasn't the truth. The best he could do was last night eating dinner in front of the fire with Sara, and this morning waking up to her lovely face and her luscious mouth and that tiny jolt of desire in her green, green eyes.

Maybe that was why he'd beat it out of there so fast this afternoon, he thought while he gazed around the hellhole he called home and compared it to the palace on Westbury Boulevard with its cool marble and thick carpets and museum-quality works of art. Not that he thought all that glitz meant much to her, but it was her customary glitz all the same. Way out of his league even when he'd been the proud owner of a three-story Victorian. Now that he resided in the black hole of Calcutta, she was more than out of his league. She was out of his universe.

He'd left her without suggesting they go out on an official date sometime partly because he didn't want to hear her say no, partly because he was hoping she'd invite him back to her sweet sanctuary for another fire-lit dinner.

Well, she didn't, did she?

*That's what happens when you take your eye off the
ball, Decker. That's what you get when you stop playing cop and start playing house, you jerk. The lady's
safe now. She doesn't need you anymore.*

What he needed was to put a good night's sleep
between himself and Sara Campbell. He shrugged out
of his shoulder holster, then didn't even bother taking
off his shoes when he slung himself out on his squeaky,
bar-across-the-backbone bed.

It was still dark when his phone jolted him awake.
Joe glanced at his watch before he answered. It was
six-thirty in the morning, which meant he'd slept about
five hours even though it felt like five minutes. He
reached for the receiver without getting up.

"Decker."

"We've got trouble, partner."

Maggie's voice made him sit straight up. "Tell me."

"It turns out our Peeping Tom was in the psych
ward at the state hospital in Bronson when the Ripper
killed victims four and five. Guess why he was in the
psych ward."

"For confessing to another crime he couldn't possibly have committed," Joe answered flatly.

"Bingo."

He swore softly into the phone.

"There's more, Joe."

"What?" He didn't like the way Maggie's voice
dropped to an ominous register.

"A woman was killed last night. About two o'clock,
the ME thinks. From the looks of it, she's victim number eight."

Joe swore again. "I'll change clothes and be right
there, Mag."

"Wait a minute. There's more. The woman was

found in the back seat of her Land Cruiser in an alley just off Ninth and Prospect. That's just—''

''A couple blocks from Sara's house.'' He finished for her even though his heart was clogging his throat. He swallowed hard. ''Maggie...''

''I know. I've already put you on today's sick list so you can get right over there. In the meantime I asked Fuller and Bristol to check in on her while they're on patrol.''

''You're a peach, Mag. Talk to you later.''

He hung up, stuffed his last clean pair of jeans and a shirt into his gym bag and was out the door in three minutes flat.

When her front doorbell rang at six forty-five, Sara was pouring herself a second cup of coffee. She shoved the pot under the drip basket and put her half-filled mug on the counter with a thud, then raced to the door, hoping it was Joe Decker, thinking that it had to be because nobody else would ring her doorbell at such an ungodly hour.

She called, ''Who is it?,'' anticipating his rich and familiar baritone in reply. *It's me, babe. Open up.* But the answer that came through the closed door wasn't what she wanted so badly to hear.

''Patrolmen Fuller and Bristol, ma'am. Just checking to see if you're okay.''

Not as okay as she'd been one second before, Sara thought bleakly. She opened the door. ''Good morning.''

The taller of the two men touched the brim of his cap. ''Morning. Sorry to disturb you. Sergeant O'Connor asked if we'd stop by and see how you're doing this morning. Is everything okay, Miss Campbell?'' He peered over her shoulder several times while he spoke, inspecting the foyer behind her.

"Everything's fine," she said. Why wouldn't it be? she wondered. With the South Side Ripper behind bars, she wasn't in jeopardy anymore. Maybe Maggie O'Connor thought Sara was such a wimp at the lineup the day before that she'd come totally unglued overnight. "I appreciate your stopping by. Thank Sergeant O'Connor for me, will you?"

"Yes, ma'am." The tall policeman, Fuller, was still peering into the foyer behind her, seemingly reluctant to leave her doorstep.

Well, maybe he just wanted a glimpse of the gaudy Campbell mansion, she thought. "Would you like to come in for a cup of coffee?" she asked. "Or could I pour you some for the road?"

"No, thanks. We…"

The sound of a souped-up engine approaching fast on Westbury drew their attention from Sara, and the cops had barely turned to look when Joe's Mustang whipped into the driveway and slid to a stop beside their patrol car. He was out of the car and trotting up the sidewalk faster than Sara's heart could turn a complete somersault.

"Hey, Lieutenant," the shorter of the two patrolmen said.

"Thanks for stopping, guys," Joe said just before his gray eyes locked on Sara. "Are you okay, Miss Campbell?"

It took a second for it to register on Sara that the formality was for the sake of their audience. "I'm fine, Lieutenant," she responded, taking the hint.

"Well, we'll take off now," Patrolman Fuller said.

"Thanks again, guys," Joe said, stepping aside to let them pass, but not taking his eyes off Sara.

"Thanks," Sara called, not taking her eyes off Joe.

They stood there, Joe on the doorstep, Sara just inside, for the longest moment. Her heart was beating so hard she thought she was having a panic attack until she suddenly realized it wasn't that at all. She was having a Decker attack.

She stepped back and he came in, closing the door behind him.

"Thank God—" he said.

"I'm so—" she said.

Their words overlapped, and the next thing Sara knew she was overlapped by the cold leather of Joe's sleeves and he was holding her so tight she almost couldn't breathe.

"You're okay," he whispered. "Damn. I should have stayed last night. I should have known."

Sara had never felt so okay in her entire life. Well, except for not being able to inhale or exhale while her rib cage was clamped in the vise of Joe's arms. She pressed her hands against his chest just a bit, easing back a few inches, lifting her face to his. "I'm so glad you came back."

There was that look again. Intense. Sensual. Heart-stopping. That gray gaze dropping to her mouth. And this time Sara was determined not to let that imminent kiss escape her. She lifted on tiptoe, whispering his name.

He made a kind of whimpering sound deep in his throat just before he lowered his head to kiss her. Then his mouth covered hers with such sheer hunger that Sara felt as if she were being consumed—by Joe, by flames, by the flood tide of desire that swept through her.

His hand moved under her sweater, cool against her burning skin, while his warm tongue teased the seam of her lips, drawing forth a little moan that Sara couldn't have stifled if she'd wanted to.

It was that unmistakable signal of surrender that seemed to bring Joe back to reality. He lifted his head, and in mere seconds Sara watched his wolfish hunger turn to sheepish remorse. He let her go, then ripped his fingers through his hair, cursing softly.

"I'm sorry. That just kind of got away from me."

Sara, whose own restraint felt harder to come by, who wasn't sorry in the least, could only imagine what might have happened if *that* had indeed gotten away from this man's fierce control.

She fashioned a wobbly smile on her wet lips. "Me, too," she said. "But I'm still glad you're back." Then she blinked. "Why *are* you back, Decker?"

Sara hadn't read the morning paper yet or listened to the news, so over coffee in the kitchen, Joe explained why he was back. The professional part, at least.

"But I thought that man I saw in the lineup yesterday had confessed," she said.

"Turns out he's a professional confessor, not to mention a nutcase." He immediately regretted his choice of words when Sara narrowed her eyes and glared at him. "No, I mean a card-carrying psycho. A *real* nutcase."

"Oh. As opposed to being an imitation one, I guess." She laughed then, just a little, before the amusement left her eyes and worry crept in. "It makes sense that I didn't recognize him, then. So, if that man wasn't the Ripper, we have to assume he's still on the loose. Right? Where was this poor woman attacked? On the South Side, again?''

Joe hadn't yet told her where the most recent victim had been discovered. He put down his coffee cup and took Sara's hand when he did. ''Three blocks from here.''

''Oh, my God,'' she breathed.

''It gets worse, I'm afraid. Her body was found in a Land Cruiser.''

It looked as if she almost stopped breathing, and it was another moment before she said, ''He thought it was me, didn't he? The Ripper thought he was killing me.''

''It looks that way.''

She pulled her hand from his and went to the coffeepot, then proceeded to pour more hot liquid onto the counter than into her cup. She just stood there shaking.

Joe took the pot from her hand, replaced it on its warmer, took her cup and put it down before she dropped it. ''I'm not going to let anything happen to you, Sara. He can't get past me to get to you. I won't let him.''

Standing behind her, he wrapped his arms around her, this time protectively, not with the outright lust he'd displayed a little while ago. Regretting that lapse in control, he whispered against her hair, ''I was out of line earlier, Sara. I'm here to protect you. That's all.''

''Well, then I was out of line, too. Don't apologize for that, Decker.'' She gave a tiny sigh, leaning her head against his shoulder. ''What are we going to do now? About the Ripper, I mean.''

"What we should do now is move you away from here." Even as he said it, he could feel her body tense against his, and he wasn't at all surprised when she said no, she wouldn't go, couldn't go. "In that case," he told her, "we just stay here and wait."

"How long will you be assigned to stay with me?" she asked.

"Assigned," he murmured, reluctant to tell her he wasn't here in an official capacity, that the department's budget wouldn't stretch to protect her life. Unwilling, too, to give her the impression that he'd rather be here with her than anyplace else in the world. "As long as it's necessary."

"That's good." She relaxed a little more against him.

"So I guess you're stuck with me, Campbell, for the duration."

"I'd say it's more like you're stuck with me, Decker." She sighed. "I'm sorry I ever pulled that man's mask off. I should have just handed him my car keys and told him to have a nice day."

"Yeah, but then I wouldn't ever have had the chance to eat green noodles and purple lettuce."

She laughed. "Oh, I see. This is all a part of your culinary destiny, then."

"Maybe." *Maybe a lot more than that.*

His destiny, Joe decided a few days later, in addition to eating weird food, was taking cold showers and doing a batch of punishing push-ups and sit-ups each night after Sara had gone to bed. After going three years without being attracted to any woman, much less turned on by one, he wasn't used to feeling like a randy teenager twenty-four hours a day.

Distracted as he was by her face and the flair of her hips and the fit of her sweaters, it was a good thing the Ripper hadn't made a move since he'd killed his eighth victim Thursday night. It was Sunday night. All quiet on the Campbell front. Well, except for the ache in Joe's groin.

He put another log on the fire, then wandered to the kitchen where Sara had disappeared a while before. From the hallway he could hear the clamor of metal pots and pans, and above that Sara humming another oldie, only slightly off key. That made him smile, but it was the unexpected sight of her with flour on her face, in her hair, all over, that made him laugh out loud.

"You look like you've been snorting coke," he said, touching the flour-dusted tip of her nose. "I might have to arrest you."

"Not until I'm done with this, Officer." She began to pour batter into a round metal pan.

"What are you doing?"

"Making a birthday cake."

He remembered that he'd read her date of birth on her driver's license and that he hoped she lived to see the ripe old age of thirty-one. Had it only been last Monday, he wondered, that Sara Campbell was merely the stats on a driver's license? In less than a week, she'd worked her way into his every waking thought, his every aching thought.

"For you?" he asked.

"For me." She was wielding a plastic spatula, coaxing the last of the batter from the bowl. "Want to come to my party tomorrow, Decker?"

"Sure. I'm assuming it's here."

"Home, sweet home." She licked a bit of batter from her finger, and Joe almost groaned at the sight.

"And who else is coming to this party?" he asked, watching her lush derriere as she bent to slide the cake pans in the oven.

"Let's see. There's me. There's you." She closed the oven door and stood up, turning to him with a grin. "That's it. A party of two."

He was absurdly relieved. "Do we get to wear funny hats and play pin the tail on the donkey?"

"No. But we get to play dress-up and drink copious amounts of champagne."

"I like the champagne part. The dress-up part isn't going to work, though, unless you have a tuxedo in my size just lying around somewhere."

She was at the sink, rinsing things. "I thought we could have one delivered from one of those rental places."

"I've got a better idea," he said. "How long does it take to bake those things?"

"About half an hour. Why?"

"You'll see."

"Decker." She shot him a suspicious look over her shoulder. "This wouldn't involve going anywhere, would it? Because if it does…"

# Chapter 8

"I really don't want to do this, Joe," Sara muttered as he backed out of her driveway. "I really, really don't want to do this."

"Well, I really, really, really do." Once on Westbury, he drove east, which wasn't the way to their destination, but he wanted to make certain they weren't being followed. Not only that, he wanted to cruise around the streets where the Ripper had cruised the night before. Since Sara didn't know where his apartment was, she would be none the wiser for the detour.

The streets were quiet on this cold Sunday evening. The snow that had fallen earlier in the week was piled high along the curbs. Joe didn't think he'd be so lucky as to see a guy wearing a ski mask out for a stroll, but if the guy had pinpointed Sara's neighborhood somehow, he might be lurking somewhere out here.

"This is where the murder happened last night," Sara said. "Isn't it?"

"Pretty close."

She shivered, then reached to make sure her door was locked. "Your door's locked, right?"

"Yes, ma'am." He didn't want to unnerve her any more than he already had, so Joe turned onto Westbury and headed southwest toward his place. Oncoming headlights revealed Sara's pale, tense face. "Relax, birthday girl. We'll pick up my tux and be back to your place in no time. Jeez, I hope it doesn't smell like mothballs. I never thought about that."

"When was the last time you wore it?"

He had to think about that a minute. Obviously it was more than three years ago, before Edie died. Then, suddenly, he remembered. It was the night she received the Woman of the Year award from the local bar association. When the memory surfaced, he expected it to be accompanied by the customary constriction in his throat. But this time it wasn't.

"I'm sorry, Joe. Forget I asked. I know the memory must be painful," Sara said.

"No. That's okay," he said, amazed that it wasn't painful at all. It was just what it was—a memory. Bittersweet, perhaps. But not painful. "The last time I wore it was to a bar association dinner just over three years ago. It's been hanging away in a garment bag ever since."

"Well, if it smells like mothballs, we'll have almost twenty-four hours to air it out. And if that doesn't work, I'll wear mosquito repellent instead of perfume, then we'll both reek."

The streets grew narrower and the buildings shabbier as they drove. Sara, he figured, had never been in this section of the city before. He drove past his building, ashamed of the way he'd let his life deteriorate, imagining she'd see something about him that he never wanted anybody to see—the disrepair of his soul. This had been a lousy idea from the start. Dammit. But he'd started it, so he might just as well finish it. He circled around the block and parked between two old rusted-out pickups in front of his redbrick hellhole.

At least somebody had swept out the leaves and candy wrappers that always blew into the dim little lobby, he thought when they entered. He sniffed the stagnant air, replete with cooking oil and decades of poorly housebroken pets.

"Second floor," he said, leading a quiet Sara up the stained, worn stairs. He paused after inserting his key in the lock of the scuffed and battered door. "Expect the worst," he said, trying to grin. "My cleaning lady quit a year and a half ago."

He gritted his teeth, turned the key and pushed in the door.

When Sara stepped over the threshold, the last thing on her mind was critiquing the decor. All she wanted to do was find a chair and sit. Her heart had begun to thump erratically as soon as she had gotten out of the car, and her head felt as light as a helium balloon. If she didn't sit down, she thought, she was going to throw up.

"I need a chair," she said, and Joe immediately began to toss things onto the floor, disclosing a tattered blue recliner. She sagged into its depths, closing her eyes to fight the onslaught of dizziness.

"Pretty bad, huh?" he said.

"I'll be all right in a minute."

"No, I meant the room."

He sounded so forlorn that Sara forgot about her distress. She opened her eyes and gazed around. It was pretty bad. No, it was worse than that. It was the saddest room she had ever seen.

"Aw, Joe," she said softly.

He gave her the oddest look. For a second it seemed he didn't recognize her at all, but then it seemed he not only recognized her but knew her better than anyone else in the world. Knew her and loved her. Her breath stalled in her throat.

"Let me find that tux and we'll get out of this dump," he said, then disappeared into another room, leaving Sara to survey the devastation of his life.

There were boxes everywhere, some of them taped closed, others disgorging their contents onto the floor. Magazines that once might have been neatly stacked slid across the carpet like so many cards and mingled with tattered books. She counted three white cartons of take-out Chinese, plastic forks still poking from their tops. She picked those up and crammed them into an already full wastebasket. She righted one skewed lampshade, then sighed and gave up. What she needed, rather than a broom and a dustpan, was a shovel and a Dumpster.

On the far side of the unmade sofa bed, Sara spied the corner of a framed photo among the clutter on a bookshelf, so she made her way around the bed to inspect it more closely. It turned out to be a picture of a wonderful Victorian house, a venerable painted lady, with scrollwork and gingerbread and balusters in varying shades of yellow and ocher. A perfect house, she thought. One that was the epitome of home, sweet home if ever she had seen one.

And sitting there on the wraparound veranda were the proud and happy owners, Mr. and Mrs. Joe Decker. The woman was petite and blond and lovely, and the man by her side was smiling in a way that Sara had never seen him smile. There was nothing roguish about it. That smile was composed of pure love. For a moment Sara ached to see a similar one.

"I found it. Let's get out of here."

Sara eased the picture onto the shelf. "I wasn't snooping," she said, feeling as if she'd just been caught spying on him. "I just…"

"No problem. Hey, at least you know I haven't always lived like this." He gave the room one last, scathing glance. "Come on. We're outta here."

His tux, as it turned out, reeked of cedar rather than mothballs. When Joe unzipped the garment bag later that evening, several heart-shaped cedar chips fell out. He held them for a moment, turning the smooth, reddish wood over in the palm of his hand, trying to imagine Edie's determined expression when she'd put the chips in the bag so long ago to foil the moths. Her image, though, refused to materialize in his brain.

It was easier somehow to picture Sara's sweet, sympathetic face at his apartment when she'd seen the staggering disarray in which he existed. He'd expected her to be horrified at the sight, or if not that, then at least completely disenchanted. That she'd been so moved by his plight and his pitiful surroundings had touched his heart. And when she'd uttered that soft, sad, "Aw, Joe," he thought he'd fallen just a little bit in love with her, if he hadn't already been.

He hadn't planned on that, he thought. If he'd planned on anything at all, it was merely spending time with her here in her cozy sanctuary, inevitably spending time—long nights and lazy mornings—in her pil-

lowy bed. Love had never entered his mind. Not once.
Until tonight.

"Very chic, Lieutenant."

Her voice startled him when she came into the room
directly across the hall from her bedroom. The cedar
chips fell from his hand into the open garment bag. Joe
lifted the tux on its thick plastic hanger.

"No moth holes," he said, inspecting the sleeves
and lapels, "but it's probably way out of style."

"Only if it has a Nehru jacket," she said with a little
laugh, "or a psychedelic cummerbund." She came
closer, sniffed, then crinkled her nose. "Maybe we
should hang it outside overnight so it doesn't smell like
a redwood forest."

"I'll do it," he said when she reached for the hanger.

"I can do it, for heaven's sake. I'm perfectly safe
out on my own back porch for one minute, Joe. Good
grief."

He didn't want to tell her that she wasn't. He didn't
want to let her know that taking the tux outside gave
him a good excuse to check around out back, to see if
there were any footprints that shouldn't be there or if
any of the threads he'd tied earlier in the day had been
disturbed.

"It's late," he said. "You should probably get some
sleep."

"I need to finish frosting the cake."

"Why don't we cheat and have a piece of it tonight
with a glass of milk?" he suggested.

"We can't do that."

Sara looked so truly appalled that it made him laugh.
"Why not?"

"Well, we just can't, that's why." Her hands fluttered at the folded collar of her turtleneck. "It's a birthday cake, and it's not my birthday yet."

Joe checked his watch. "Almost. Another ninety minutes."

Her lush lips firmed, and she crossed her arms. "No. Absolutely not. And don't you dare sneak a piece, either, Decker. I mean it."

"What's the big deal?"

"I don't know, but it is a big deal. It upsets my sense of order, I guess." She grinned. "And it's against regulations."

"Ah. Well, far be it from me to go against those." He covered his heart with his hand, then reached out to skim a finger along her cheek. "I like your sense of order, you know. I could use some of that in my life right now."

"I noticed," she said softly.

She leaned into his touch like a cat, causing Joe's heart to beat harder and his blood to take a decidedly southward turn. There was no order in what he was feeling, only an urgency he hadn't experienced in years, and along with that a tenderness he didn't even know he was capable of.

"You're distracting as hell, you know that, Campbell?"

Her big green eyes shone merrily when they lifted to his. "Is that good or bad, Lieutenant?"

"I'll have to think about that. Can I get back to you?"

"Absolutely. I'll be the one in the kitchen, licking frosting off my fingers."

Sara was doing just that when Joe came into the kitchen along with a cold blast of air. When he eyed her cake greedily, she shoved him away with her hip.

"Oh, no, you don't," she said. "Here. This is all you get." She held up her right ring finger, still gooey with white icing.

His fingers circled her wrist like a warm bracelet, then instead of merely licking the frosting, he took her finger in his mouth and gently sucked. Sara's heart slammed against her ribs so hard she thought she was going to pass out. She reached out her left hand to steady herself and promptly gouged a wide swath in the side of her cake.

"Damn," she whispered.

Joe released her finger. "What?"

"Now you're distracting *me,*" she exclaimed, licking icing from her left hand while pointing with her right to the wounded cake. "I don't have any icing left to fix it, either."

He grinned. "Well, in that case, let's just eat it."

Sara slapped his hand. "Don't you dare. What happened to that order you were craving, Decker?"

"I lost my head."

"Obviously," she said with a little snort as she picked up the cake and moved it out of harm's way.

"Sara." He was standing close behind her when he spoke her name with a huskiness that sent a little ripple of desire along her spine. "Sara," he said again, moving closer, so close that she could feel the heat of him penetrating the back of her sweater, feel his breath on her neck.

He put his hands on her shoulders, lodged his chin in the crook of her neck. "This is going to happen, you know. Us. Sooner or later."

She knew, but all she could do was nod.

"But later's better than sooner, under the circumstances." He circled his arms around her. "I don't want to let down my guard, and I would if we..."

"I know," she answered with a soft sigh. "I keep forgetting this is work for you. I keep forgetting about *him.*"

"We can't afford to forget." He nuzzled her ear. "But don't think for one second that you're just a job to me. I want you, Sara. I haven't felt like this about anybody in a long time."

"Neither have I." She could hardly speak for the sensations that were coursing from her ear throughout her body. "I never expected this to happen."

He chuckled, his breath warm against her neck. "Well, I guess if the Ripper's ever done anything good in his whole worthless life, it's this."

Sara stood there, letting Joe's warmth surround her, absorbing it into her very soul, amazed that someone seemed to care so much and at the same time more than a little afraid, wondering how something so good could have been born of a murderer's evil.

Maggie stopped by early the next morning on her way to the station. Her blond hair looked a bit disheveled and her Irish smile didn't pack its usual pizzazz. Joe poured her a cup of coffee.

"Sorry this is all falling on your shoulders, Mag," he said, leaning against the counter while Maggie took a seat at the island. "I've got to stay here, though."

"You're getting awfully comfortable here, aren't you, Decker?" she asked, eyeing him over the rim of her cup. "A little too comfortable, maybe?"

"She's a nice lady." That was about all Joe was willing to disclose about his comfort level at the moment, and his partner knew him well enough to let the subject drop. "What's going on down at the store?"

"No prints turned up in the new victim's car," Maggie said, "but you probably already suspected that. The ME's doing the autopsy this morning, but he's already ninety-nine percent sure that the Ripper's our guy on this one." She took another sip of her coffee. "Oh, yeah, and Cobble's getting pretty suspicious about this sudden lingering illness of yours."

"Let him. I haven't taken a sick day in seven or eight years. He might be willing to risk a witness's life, but I'm not."

"I take it the nice lady hasn't remembered anything yet?"

Joe shook his head. "She dreamed about him the other night, but blanked out on the face after she woke up." When Maggie gave him the fish eye, he added, "Alone."

"What do you want me to tell Cobble?" she asked.

"Tell him anything you want. Tell him I'm keeping his goddamn witness alive so he doesn't have another murder on the books. Tell him to go—"

"Good morning," Sara said, appearing in the doorway. "If I'm interrupting something, I can come back."

Maggie stood up. "Good morning. Hey, it's your kitchen. I was just stopping by on my way to work to see how things are going."

"As well as can be expected, I guess." Sara glanced at Joe, as if for confirmation, or perhaps to glean what, if anything, he had told his partner about how *things* were going.

"Happy birthday," he said, trying to keep a note of intimacy out of his tone when all he wanted to do was wrap Sara in his arms and kiss her until she couldn't breathe and make this the best birthday of her life.

She smiled, walked toward the coffeepot. "Thanks. I almost forgot."

"Congratulations," Maggie said. She drained the last of her coffee and put her cup down. "Well, I've gotta go check in."

"Let me know when the autopsy report comes in, Mag."

"Will do."

Joe let Maggie out the back door but wasn't quick enough to escape one last squinty-eyed perusal from her or a final warning, uttered sotto voce. "You be careful, partner."

"Be careful about what?" Sara asked when he came back.

"Nothing." He shrugged.

She raised a skeptical brow. "Joe? Be careful about what?"

"You."

"Me!" Sara exclaimed.

"Maggie's a detective, remember? I think she detected a rise in my blood pressure when you came in the room."

"Was she right?"

He folded his fingers around his wrist and ticked off fifteen seconds on his watch, then multiplied by four, then grinned. "Yeah. A definite rise. This could be serious."

"Well, I think I might have a cure for that," she said.

"Does it involve lips, by any chance?"

"Most definitely." With a smile worthy of the Mona Lisa, she went to the refrigerator. "I think we should have birthday cake for breakfast, Decker. What do you think?''

''Breakfast! Cake? Where's your sense of order, Campbell?''

''Gone, apparently.''

She laughed as she ran her finger along the edge of the cake, then offered the sweet clump of frosting on her fingertip to Joe.

Sara's sense of order was definitely out of whack for the better part of the day. She could hardly concentrate on business, so she turned off her computer shortly after noon and went downstairs to begin preparing her birthday dinner of veal piccata and penne with Swiss chard and pine nuts. While she was washing the big, dark green leaves of chard under the faucet, the front doorbell rang.

''Joe,'' she called, knowing he didn't want her to answer the door under any circumstances but not knowing if he'd heard the bell.

When it rang again, she shut off the faucet and dried her hands on a towel while she trotted to the door. To her surprise, Joe was already there.

''Why didn't you open it?'' she asked, suddenly a little fearful of what or who might be on the other side.

''It's for you,'' he said.

Sara narrowed her eyes. ''What do you mean?''

''Go ahead. Open it.''

More curious than alarmed, Sara tossed him the damp towel, then opened the door to a young delivery boy holding an large rectangular box.

''Flowers for Miss Sara Campbell,'' he said.

''Oh, gosh!'' It probably wasn't the most sophisticated greeting the boy had ever received, but it was the first thing that came into her head. It had been a long time since anyone had sent her flowers. "Oh, my goodness."

The boy put the long white box in her outstretched arms. "There you go, ma'am. Enjoy."

A hand emerged from behind her with a crisply folded bill.

"Thanks a lot," Joe said to him.

After Sara angled the long box through the door, Joe took it from her, saying, "Let me see that for just a sec."

"What are you going to do? Inspect it for a bomb?" she asked. He was squatting on the marble floor of the foyer, untying the box's big red bow, taking off the lid, then riffling through the green tissue while muttering to himself.

"Joe? What in the world are you doing?"

"What I'm doing," he muttered, "is making this right. Ouch. Dammit."

He brought his thorn-stuck thumb to his mouth for a second, then plunged it in the box. Then, one by one, he pulled out five long-stemmed roses and tossed them aside.

"What are you doing?" Sara asked. Was he crazy? Did he really think those gorgeous roses were some insidious trick of the Ripper?

He put the lid on the box, retied the bow, then stood up. "Happy birthday, Sara." He put the box in her arms again.

She looked at the box, then at the five discarded blooms, then at the pleased grin on Joe's face. "Help me out here, Decker."

"Thirty-one roses," he said, "for your thirty-first birthday."

"But…"

"The battle-ax on the phone at the florist's refused to sell me the thirty-one roses I wanted. They only sold them by the dozen. Period. Policy. Regulations. So I said okay, fine, no problem, charge me for three dozen, but put thirty-one in the damn box. No. She couldn't do that."

Sara started laughing at the exasperation on his face and in his voice.

"Okay, I told her. Here's what you do. Put three dozen roses in the box, then take out five. Well, then she got kind of huffy and wanted to know what she was supposed to do with those five. And I got even more huffy and told her just what she could do with them." He sighed. "I was actually pretty surprised they arrived at all, to tell you the truth."

She hugged the box. "This is the best birthday present I've ever gotten. Thank you for going to so much trouble."

"You're welcome." He sucked on his wounded thumb again. "Just watch those thorns. I think my friend at the florist's chose the sharpest ones she could find."

Dinner was at eight in the huge, walnut-paneled dining room with its White House sized crystal chandelier and inlaid table only slightly smaller than Rhode Island. Even thirty-one roses in a tall crystal vase looked puny in comparison.

Sara had done her best to make it intimate by setting their places at a corner of the big table. And by some miracle that Joe figured he'd never begin to comprehend, she had come up with a dress that was the exact color and texture of the roses. The rich velvety crimson scooped low at the neckline, then caressed her breasts and hips before flowing to the floor. She wore a bit more makeup than usual, Joe noticed, making her eyes a deeper green, framed by thick, dark lashes, and she'd done something shiny and alluring with her hair. Every once in a while a diamond would sparkle at one of her ears.

She looked so beautiful, so ravishing that he could hardly take his eyes off her, and he ate his Swiss chard obediently, without a single snide comment or complaint, all the while hoping that the aftershave he'd used before he dressed was strong enough to mask the cedar stench of his tux.

"Thank you for the roses," she said for what had to be the twentieth time, then added, "my father used to have roses delivered to my mother on the tenth of every month to celebrate the day they met, but I don't think they were ever as lovely as these."

"Sounds like a pretty romantic guy," Joe said, wondering if Campbell had ever given his daughter so much as a daisy.

"He was. My mother adored him. Well, they adored each other." She took a sip of her wine, which, by some other miracle Joe couldn't fathom, also matched the roses perfectly.

"And where did little Sara fit into the equation?" he asked.

Putting her wineglass down with deliberation, she looked at him with those frank green eyes. "I didn't, really. Oh, they loved me in their own way. They bought me tons of clothes and toys and stuff. More than I ever needed or wanted. But it was pretty much just the two of them. I was..." Her voice drifted off with her gaze.

"Just a blip on the screen of their great romance?" he suggested, a little more acid in his voice than he'd intended.

"Something like that."

Her smile was so sad it made Joe want to break something. Either that or take her in his arms and tell her that it would be so easy for somebody to shower her with the love and attention that her parents never did. Somebody like him.

"You deserved better, babe," he said. "I should take you to meet my parents one of these days. They had nine kids and love enough for—" He stopped mid-sentence, put down his fork and blinked.

"What? What's wrong?"

He muttered a little curse, then said, "I was thinking so much about your birthday that I completely forgot this is the night of their big anniversary bash."

"Oh, Joe." She stared at him with a mixture of sympathy and mounting anxiety on her pretty face, no doubt anticipating—dreading, actually—what he was going to say next.

"Sorry, babe." He folded his napkin, tucked it under his plate, then pushed back his chair. "We have to go."

# Chapter 9

Joe rolled his eyes and let out a sigh when the little redbrick house on Pearl Avenue came into view. It wasn't even Thanksgiving yet, but the house where he'd grown up was decked out from rooftop to porch floor in thousands of multicolored Christmas lights. He'd taken a circuitous route from the Campbell house just to make sure they hadn't been followed, so it probably seemed to Sara that the Decker house was farther away than it really was. On the other hand, he thought, this three-bedroom brick bungalow was about as far as anybody could get from the mansion on Westbury Boulevard.

The driveway was crammed with cars, so he eased the Mustang alongside the curb behind his brother Mike's Blazer.

"Merry Christmas," he said, turning off the ignition, nodding toward the brightly decorated house. "My mother rushes the season more every year. Pretty soon she'll have my dad out stringing lights on Labor Day.''

Sara's response was a tight, almost brittle smile. In the warm glow of the Christmas lights, Joe could see that she looked pale and scared to death. It probably wasn't helping that the car smelled like a funeral parlor from the roses she'd insisted he bring as a gift for his parents. He cracked the window open an inch, slipped an arm around the back of her seat, then reached for her hand.

"This will only take a minute. I promise."

"I'll wait here for you, okay?"

"If you do, my mother's going to be coming down the sidewalk in about three minutes with a big welcome smile on her face and a hot toddy in her hand, followed by my dad with a plate of hors d'oeuvres, and one or two sisters…"

"Please," she said. "I just can't do this, Joe. My heart's already going ninety miles an hour."

"Try that special breathing you said your shrink recommended."

"It isn't helping," she wailed. "And distracting myself from my damn panic isn't working, either."

"Maybe you're not distracted enough," he said.

"What do you mean?"

"This."

His right hand cupped her shoulder and pulled her closer while his left hand came up to cradle her face, then he kissed her the way he'd been wanting to do all evening. All week. Her lips tensed in surprise for a moment and then relaxed beneath the soft pressure of his mouth as if she'd been waiting just as long as he had for this, as if she wanted it just as much as he did.

"Sara," he breathed before deepening the kiss and

tasting her, all wine and birthday cake and musky roses. Before he knew what he was doing, his hand slipped beneath the cloak she wore, seeking the warmth of her velvet-covered breast. She moaned softly while his thumb drifted back and forth across its peak, while his tongue sampled the sweet depths of her mouth.

Joe could feel her heart beating beneath his hand, but it wasn't the wild tattoo of panic anymore. It was the solid, sensuous cadence of desire, and it matched his own heart, beat for beat. He was sorely tempted to start the car and race to her house, to her pillowy bed.

Instead he broke the kiss and drew back his hand. The car windows were steamed up, making the Christmas lights little more than a multicolored blur. He put his head on the seat back and blew out a breath.

"I don't know about you, Campbell, but that just distracted the hell out of me."

"Me, too," she said softly.

"Look. I'll leave this up to you. I'd really like to see my folks on their anniversary, but if you want to go home, that's okay, too. I'll just give them a call and tell them I can't get away from work."

She chewed on her lower lip a moment, then muttered decisively, "Let's go."

"Home?"

"No. Here." She opened her door. "And you better move fast, Decker, before I lose my nerve and change my mind."

He snatched the roses from the back seat and met her on the sidewalk, sliding his arm around her waist and urging her gently toward the house. Ahead, he could see several curtains being pulled back and one or two slats of venetian blinds being pried apart. God help her, he thought. Sara Campbell was about to be Deckered.

If Sara had longed to be distracted from her palpitating heart and her clammy hands, then the Decker house was the perfect place to be distracted. At least a hundred people—and at times it seemed more like a thousand—had gathered to help Rose and Mike Decker celebrate their wedding anniversary. There were big people with hearty handshakes and hugs. There were little people—girls in velvet dresses and lace collars, boys in plaid bow ties—giggling and spilling punch and filling paper plates with cake and brownies and mixed nuts. There were sisters and brothers and in-laws and neighbors and swirls of cousins and uncles and aunts.

The little house was bursting with people. Happy people so in contrast to those who attended the parties her parents used to give, where everyone looked either suspicious or bored. And little people having just as good a time, if not better, than the grown-ups. When there were parties at her house, she used to be fed her dinner early and put to bed before the first guest arrived. Later, when she was older, she was expected to have a proper escort and to look as suitably bored as everyone else. She usually was.

It was a bit like being swept along in a victory parade after a football game. And if Sara couldn't quite keep track of who was who, the one thing she knew was that Joe's strong arm was constantly around her, and every minute on the minute, he was searching her face with his intense gray eyes and whispering "Are you okay, babe?"

Actually, she was pretty okay. The smile on her face

wasn't one of those painful, plastic ones. Her voice, when she heard it above the general din, was level and calm. Her hands weren't shaking. Well, not so much that she couldn't bring a glass of punch to her lips without fear of spilling it. It was amazing, really. She'd gone for probably five or ten minutes without even thinking about fainting or fleeing in sheer panic, and she'd managed to focus on others instead of herself for a blessed change.

"Are you okay, babe?"

Joe was gazing at her, holding her even closer against his side. He had maneuvered her to the only quiet corner of the jam-packed living room.

"Fine," she said.

"Honest?"

Sara nodded. "I haven't even considered fainting, and we've been here, what? At least fifteen minutes now."

Joe checked his watch. "More like forty-five minutes. And, hell, if you fainted in here, there'd be no place to fall down." He grinned. "To tell you the truth, the noise is starting to get to me a little bit. I think we should—"

A speeding ball of yellow fur, dragging a long red leash, cut between their feet, only to disappear in the opposite direction. A second after that, a tiny girl in a red velvet dress rammed into Sara's legs, looked up, said, "Oops," then disappeared in the same direction as the puppy. Hard on the little girl's Mary Jane heels was a woman with eyes the exact gray of Joe's.

"Joey," she said with a beleaguered sigh, "will you do me a favor, please, and catch my wild child and that blasted animal before they knock somebody down?"

"Sure, Lissie." He handed her his punch glass. "Take care of my date, okay? Don't let her escape."

He disappeared in the throng of people. Sara, left to fend for herself, felt a little twinge of panic rush through her. Date? His *date?*

"Sara, right?" the woman asked her.

"Yes."

"I'm Melissa, Joey's big sister, and I promise you it isn't always quite this much of a madhouse around here."

"I'm enjoying it," Sara said.

"Have you met everybody?" She laughed. "No, of course you haven't. But you will eventually. So, how long have you known Joey?"

"About a week now."

Melissa edged a little bit closer, then lifted Joe's punch glass in a kind of toast. "Well, I'd like to congratulate you on achieving the impossible."

"What's that?"

"Making my brother smile again. We're grateful." Melissa gestured across the crowded room. "All of us. Especially my mom and dad. Joey's been hurting for such a long time and nothing any of us did seemed to help all that much."

The incipient panic in Sara's heart melted from the warmth in the woman's voice and her obvious sincerity. "He's lucky to have such a loving family," she said.

"Yes, I guess he is. But right now I'd say he's even luckier to have you."

Sara didn't know what to say, but before she could reply, Joe was back, a giggling niece under one arm and a squirming puppy under the other.

"Here go you, Sis." He deposited them in Melissa's

arms, then kissed her cheek. "We're going to make a quiet escape out the back door. Cover for us, will you?"

"Sure." She winked at Sara. "Thanks again. I mean it."

Joe took Sara's hand and began to thread through the maze of people. "What was Lissie thanking you for?" he asked.

"Oh, just the roses," Sara said.

And before they managed to make their escape, Sara heard whispered thanks from two more sisters and at least three brothers. There was a warm embrace from Joe's mother. But best of all was the giant bear hug from Joe's father when the big man whispered brokenly, "It's good to see my son happy again."

All the way home Joe regaled Sara with family stories, partly because he loved the sound of her laughter, mostly because—for the first time in a long time—he wanted to share them. It hadn't escaped his notice that just about everyone at the party had been whispering behind his back about this sudden and unexpected appearance with a woman after three years of coming home sullen and solo.

He kept thinking how happy Sara had looked after she'd gotten used to the crush and the noise in the little house. His big, boisterous family had done her a world of good, he thought, and she hadn't given him the least indication that she felt she was slumming. Hell, if nothing else, it was a step up from his ramshackle pad.

In her driveway, he turned the engine off and watched Sara a minute while she gazed at the big house, wondering what was going through her head. Was his little recluse relieved to be about to retreat to her sanctuary again? Was she glad it wasn't dripping with premature Christmas lights and full of people drinking punch and beer? "Home, sweet home," he said.

Her sigh didn't give him much of a clue to her thoughts. "I had fun tonight, Joe," she said. "Thank you."

"Good. We can do it again on a smaller scale, if you want. I guess you heard my mother invite you for Thanksgiving."

"We'll see," she said.

It sounded more like no than maybe, and suddenly Joe experienced a kind of panic of his own. He had the feeling Sara was slipping away from him now that her sanctuary was in view, and he didn't want to let her go. He didn't want to lose her. Not to the Ripper. Not to another man. Not even to this house. It was all he could do not to pull her into his arms and kiss her and touch her and love her until she begged him not to stop. That was the problem, though. Whether she begged him or not, he wouldn't be able to stop. Under the circumstances, with the Ripper out there somewhere, that was risking far too much.

"It's getting cold out here," he said, blowing on his fingertips. "Let's go inside."

They walked up the sidewalk arm in arm. It felt natural, but Joe hoped a patrol car didn't come by and give everybody down at the precinct tomorrow's hot gossip. He recalled Maggie's caution this morning. What if he was falling in love with Sara? he asked himself. He was a big boy. He could handle it. And if she didn't reciprocate his feelings, well, he knew how to handle hurt, too.

In the den, he shrugged out of the jacket of his tux,

undid his cummerbund and adjusted his shoulder holster. Sara had gone upstairs to change, so he slung himself on the couch in front of the cold fireplace. It was probably too late to light a fire, he thought, then chuckled about the other fire that had been flaring up in him all evening, the fire it was too early for.

He must have dozed off for a few minutes, because the next thing he knew Sara was brushing his hair off his forehead as she knelt beside him.

"Too much partying," she said softly. "Why don't you come upstairs and get some sleep?"

He smiled into her deep green eyes and murmured, "So, Campbell, are you going to be the kind of mother who wakes a kid who's sound asleep on the couch and tells him to go to bed?"

"Probably."

"It's your sense of order, right?"

She laughed. "Well, beds are for sleeping."

"Yeah." He brought her fingers to his lips for a kiss. "Among other things that I don't even want to think about right now."

"Too distracting?" she whispered.

"Much."

"Then come upstairs and just hold me, Joe."

"I have a better idea." He shifted onto his side and toward the back of the couch, then patted the empty space in front of him. "You come up here."

When she did there was just enough time to glimpse the sheer gown she was wearing beneath her loosely tied silk robe. She burrowed against him, her head in the crook of his shoulder, her backside warm against his crotch. "This is nice," she said with a sleepy sigh that turned into a yawn. "I'm warning you, Joe. I could fall sound asleep right here."

"Go ahead, babe."

"Really? Will you be comfortable?"

He stroked her soft hair. "Yeah. No problem."
*Yeah. Right.*

The problem arose when she grew restless in her sleep and flopped over so they were lying face-to-face.

"I thought you were a quiet sleeper," Joe grumbled softly, edging back a little more and tucking in his chin, the better to see her pretty face, her long soft lashes, her mouth relaxed in sleep.

He smoothed his hand along her silk-covered arm, over her silken flank where her robe and gown had ridden above her knee.

"You're not making this any easier for me, Campbell," he whispered. "You know that, don't you?"

Reaching up, he smoothed a few stray curls from her face, smiling as he did so. It was the kind of smile that seemed to float from his heart all of its own accord. A goofy smile, he thought. A helium balloon with a happy face on it.

Okay. So he was in love for the second time in his life. And this time with a woman who was so different from his first love that he hardly knew how to compare the two. He searched Sara's sleeping face, looking for physical traces of Edie, finding no resemblance at all. Edie's features were sharp, intense, from her perfectly delineated eyebrows to her high cheekbones and sharply defined chin. Sara's features were soft. A kitten to Edie's cat.

A very distracting kitten, too. By God, if he didn't bring the Ripper in soon, he was going to be a physical and emotional wreck. Not only that, but if he didn't get back to his regular work at the precinct house, he was going to be up for suspension, or worse, termination.

Dammit. He almost wished the Ripper would make a move tonight, right this minute, so he could put an end to him. What was he waiting for?

It suddenly occurred to him that maybe the Ripper hadn't been around because he thought he'd been successful in killing his only witness the other night. Joe had been going on the theory that it had been quiet at the Campbell house because the Ripper was waiting. Maybe, though, just maybe the son of a bitch had quit.

If it hadn't been for Sara in his arms, Joe would have been up and on the phone that instant because he already knew what his next move would have to be in order for the Ripper to find out he hadn't killed the star witness after all. But it could wait a few hours, he supposed.

Leaning forward, he kissed the tip of Sara's nose, then whispered, "Sleep well, babe. This is going to get a lot worse before it's over and done with." Then he closed his eyes to store up some sleep in preparation for the coming fireworks.

The fireworks began around five o'clock the next day when Sara read the afternoon edition of the *Daily Express.* It was another gray day with sleet giving way to a light but steady snow. Joe was just putting another log on the fire when Sara, snuggled in her usual corner of the couch, bolted upright and snapped the newspaper like a whip, then wailed, "I don't believe this!"

Bingo, he thought, before he pivoted on the balls of his feet, turning to her, innocently asking, "Hmm? What's wrong?"

"This!" She stabbed a finger at the lower right corner of the front page where Evan Cormack's "By the Way" column appeared three times a week. "Cormack says that I can identify the Ripper. Listen to this. 'Sources in the police department have revealed that their witness, in concert with renowned FBI sketch artist John Ferris, was able to come up with an extremely detailed likeness of the serial killer.'" She snapped the paper again. "What sources? How can he say that? It's nothing but an outright lie."

"Let me see." Joe took the paper and read Cormack's column. It hit just the right note, he thought. He owed Cormack, big time. In the past, a case of the journalist's favorite single malt Scotch had always sufficed, but Joe was pretty sure he'd have to come up with more than a dozen bottles of liquor for this little piece of fakery in pursuit of truth and justice.

"This is outrageous," Sara said, grabbing the paper and glaring at it. "I've got a good mind to call this Cormack guy and dare him to tell me just who these sources of his are."

"That's probably not such a good idea," he said.

"Why not? He shouldn't be allowed to get away with a lie like this." She slapped the paper again.

"Maybe Cormack doesn't know it's a lie," Joe suggested.

"You're saying somebody in your department actually passed that information along to him?"

"Maybe."

Sara snorted. "What idiot would do a thing like that?"

"Me."

Her mouth dropped open, snapped shut, then opened again with an astonished "You!" Her eyes were so wide he could see the white beneath the deep green irises. "You told this Cormack person I can identify the Ripper?"

Joe nodded.

"Why, for God's sake? That can only..." Sara's sentence sputtered out, like a hot flame in a chilling gust of wind.

He calmly finished the sentence for her. "That can only let him know he killed the wrong woman, and that his witness is still alive and well and in full possession of her memory."

Having heard that, she shot up from the couch, nearly toppling Joe, and began to pace back and forth in front of the fire. "That's crazy," she exclaimed. "You might as well have taken out a full page ad in the *Express*. Available—one witness for stabbing, raping or simple killing. Call Sara at five, five, five, oh, two, oh, two. Joe, my God! That makes me nothing more than..." Her arms flailed as she searched for a word.

"Bait?" he asked.

"Yes, well, that's a good way of putting it. Or a worm on a hook. Or a piece of cheese in a trap." She stopped pacing and fisted her hands, ramming them against her hips. "Why would you do that to me? I thought you wanted to keep me safe?"

"I do," he said. "Come here." He reached up, clamping a hand over one of her white-knuckled fists, then drawing her onto his lap. Her whole body was as tense and tight as piano wire. Beneath that, though, he could feel a deep vibrato of trembling. She was scared to death. Well, hell. She had every right to be.

"Sara, sweetheart," he said softly, "he can't get to you while I'm here. I told you that. You're safe with me. You've got to trust me."

Her soggy little sniffle didn't strike him as an overwhelming vote of confidence, so he tipped her chin and made her look deep into his eyes.

"I will not let anything happen to you. Do you understand that?" When she didn't respond, he roughened his voice. "Do you?"

She nodded, the movement shaking loose a tear from one glossy eye. "Yes, but..."

"But," Joe continued firmly, "I can't stay here indefinitely. There's going to come a time in the next week or so, maybe sooner, when my boss is going to put the screws to me and tell me either I get back to my desk or hand in my shield. I won't have a choice, babe. My job's important to me." He felt his mouth slide into a kind of grimace. "I don't know how to do anything else. I don't *want* to do anything else."

"I understand."

"What you don't understand, though, is that I can't leave you until I know you're absolutely safe. So that means that I've got to flush this son of a bitch out of the woodwork as soon as possible. And that meant I somehow had to let him know that you can ID him and put you away forever. I had to put you at risk now, Sara, while I'm here to protect you. I didn't have any choice."

Still on his lap, her face close to his, Sara was regarding him with an intense curiosity. That was when Joe realized the burning in his eyes had nothing to do with smoke from the fireplace but rather was the result of a hot sheen of moisture that had suddenly materialized there. *I'll be damned,* he thought. *Tears.* They were a good indication of just how thoroughly, how deeply this woman had gotten under his skin. He was afraid for her life. Maybe even more, at the moment, he was afraid his voice would crack if he attempted to say anything else, so he cleared his throat instead, averting his gaze from Sara's face to stare into the flames.

"I understand," she said, her voice barely more than a whisper as she nestled closer against his chest. "And I trust you, Joe. Completely."

After a minute, when he was in control of his throat again, he said, "Maybe you shouldn't."

"Why?"

"Well, maybe I have another reason for wanting to bring this Ripper business to an end. An ulterior motive, maybe."

She drew back her head enough to fix him with her green, green eyes. "Such as?"

"Such as wanting to make love to you without having to keep my eyes open and one ear on the door."

She didn't bat an eye. Didn't even laugh nervously the way he thought she might have done. She just said, "Well, then, let's bring the son of a bitch down just as fast as we can."

# Chapter 10

It was a good thing Maggie beeped him after Sara's declaration or he might have forgotten all about the danger of the Ripper while he concentrated instead on the sweet peril of a warm and willing mouth. But when his ever-present pager squealed, Joe broke the kiss with a whispered expletive, moved Sara off his lap and stalked to the phone on the desk.

"Yeah, Mag," he said, hoping his partner didn't notice the husky edge to his voice when she answered.

When the first thing out of her mouth was, "What the hell are you doing, Decker?" he knew she didn't mean kissing Sara Campbell's exquisite lips. "You read the paper," he said. It was a statement rather than a question.

"Cobble read the paper," she exclaimed, "and he's on his way over there as we speak, you idiot. Where do you get off telling Cormack what you did? Are you nuts?"

"I'm just trying to shake things up a little," Joe said.

"Well, guess what? You did." She slammed her receiver down in a blatant attempt to deafen him.

He wasn't deaf enough, though, not to hear the squeal of tires, followed by a warning blip of a siren in the driveway. The captain must have shattered the speed limit all the way from the precinct to Westbury Boulevard, Joe thought.

"That's for me," he said to Sara. He ran his thumb across his mouth just in case there was a trace of Chocolate Silk, then he raked his fingers through his hair. "I'll be right back."

Joe opened the front door, unsurprised that Frank Cobble remained in his car, thus requiring his lieutenant to come to him. The captain liked to play those subtle little power games. The jerk.

He had steamed up the windows, and when Joe opened the passenger door, a cloud of unfiltered smoke rolled out. The no-smoking ban for department vehicles never did apply to three-pack Frank.

Joe offered him a grin he knew would bug the hell out of him. "Hey, Captain."

"Get in."

After he did, Cobble waved a newspaper in his face. "What the hell is this, Decker? What's all this bullshit about a firm ID? You were supposed to tell me the minute the Campbell woman came up with anything."

"And I will, Captain," Joe said. "Cross my heart."

The man's entire face seemed to pinch tight. His thin lips closed over his cigarette. His eyes slitted against the smoke before he blew a poisonous stream in Joe's direction. "You bastard," he snarled. "She hasn't come up with a thing, has she?"

"Nope," Joe said affably. "I just thought it was

time to light a fire under our guy. Cormack seemed like a good way to do it.''

The captain breathed out an oath along with more smoke. ''You thought. *You* thought. Did you think about running the idea by me first? Did you think it might be a good idea to keep your superiors apprised in the most high-profile case we've had since the Bettman kidnapping? Or didn't that occur to you, Decker? Huh? Or have you just been too busy licking the candy heiress to—''

''Knock it off, Frank.''

Joe's voice was so low, so lethal, that Cobble's mouth fell open. Slack. Mute. That only lasted for a moment, though, before the man regained his normal nasty composure.

''I ought to write you up for that, Lieutenant.''

''Be my guest.''

''Get out of here,'' Cobble growled. ''You do one more thing that makes me look like I don't know my elbow from my ass and I'll serve *your* ass up to Internal Affairs so fast you won't know what hit you.''

Joe opened the door and got out, drawing in a deep lungful of cold, clean air. He had barely closed the passenger door before the captain threw the car in Reverse and shot onto Westbury.

''See ya in the papers, Frank,'' he muttered as he headed toward the warmth of Sara's sanctuary.

Sara couldn't do much more than stare at her computer's monitor and chew on her bottom lip, wondering who Joe was talking to in the driveway and just how long it would be before the Ripper read the paper and realized he'd murdered the wrong woman. She wondered, too, how long it would take him to find the right woman. Her.

She thought back over the past week or so, the days that seemed to have changed her life completely. Dr. Bourne had told her not to let her universe shrink to the space of a couple of rooms. It appeared that she'd inadvertently complied with the psychiatrist's suggestion. Her universe hadn't just expanded. It had exploded to include Saint Cat's, the police station, Joe's pathetic apartment and his parents' cozy little home on Pearl Street. And at the very center of that unexpected, expansive universe, smack-dab in the middle, there was Joe.

Sara couldn't have said exactly when she'd fallen in love with him. Certainly not when he'd called her a nutcase, she thought. Maybe it was when she'd gone to his apartment and been so touched by its disarray. Or maybe when he'd been so solicitous of her at his parents' party. Probably it was the first time he kissed her and she realized she never wanted him to stop.

Whenever it was, though, she wished she could take back the moment and steel herself to the emotions that had overwhelmed her. Falling in love with Joe Decker was about the dumbest thing she'd ever done in her life. No. The dumbest thing was believing, even for a second, that a woman like her had any kind of a future with a man like that.

They were as different as it was possible for two humans to be. Day and night. Apples and oranges. Alpha and beta. Active and passive. That other, age-old significant difference—male and female—was compelling but surely wasn't enough to compensate for the fact that she and Joe had nothing in common except the South Side Ripper and an overwhelming desire to collide in bed.

Out in the driveway she heard a car door slam, then the front door opened and closed and soon there were lithe footsteps coming up the stairs. For a bleak second, she almost wished it were the Ripper, come to put her out of her misery.

"Are you working?" Joe asked from the doorway.

"Sort of," she said, then sighed. "No, not really. I can't seem to concentrate."

"Not surprising." He was behind her chair, and his hands were doing incredible things to her shoulders and the muscles of her neck. "Does that help?"

"Mmm." Sara closed her eyes. They weren't focusing, anyway.

"You're tight," he murmured while his thumbs tracked down her spine, sending ripples of warmth through her entire body. Funny, she didn't feel tight at all. More like vanilla pudding. Or a stick of butter left out in direct sunlight. A puddle of sensations. Silly Putty in Decker's hands.

"Mm." It was the most intelligent thing she could say at the moment, since her brain had acquired the consistency and relative IQ of an oyster.

He was kneading the muscles at the small of her back. "I've got an idea," he said, allowing her mollusk of a brain to conjure up images of the two of them amid the pillows on her bed before he added, "tonight I'll fix dinner for you."

Dinner? Decker was thinking about food while his hands were playing her like a violin? She should probably be grateful, she told herself, that one of them had a little self-control.

"That would be nice," she said even though she wasn't the least bit hungry. Well, not for dinner, anyway.

They ate dinner in the den, their plates on the big oak coffee table, their legs folded Indian-style beneath it. Joe had forbidden Sara to come anywhere near the kitchen while he was cooking—a loud process punctuated by the slamming of drawers and more than a few heartfelt curses—because he'd wanted to surprise her. And surprise her he did. It was one of the best meals Sara had ever eaten.

"You had this brought in from Mama Savona's, didn't you?" she asked him after her last bite of the delicious, perfectly al dente pasta with its rich and creamy garlic sauce. "Come on, Decker. 'Fess up. All that banging of pots and pans I kept hearing was just subterfuge, wasn't it?"

He looked mortally wounded. "What makes you think I can't put together a decent meal, Campbell?"

"I've seen your apartment, remember?" Sara laughed. "Anyway, this is the house salad from Mama Savona's. You can't fool me. It's the best salad in town."

"Ssh." He put his fingers to his lips. "It's a secret."

"I know it's a secret. I've tried to duplicate that dressing for years and I haven't even gotten close."

"Well, then, you should have married a Savona, like I did."

The fact that he winked when he made the remark didn't prevent Sara from noticing that his eyes had turned a deeper, more melancholy gray.

"Oh, Joe. I'm sorry. I didn't know. I never meant—"

"Sara," he said, almost sternly, "it's been three years. Anyway, it's sugar."

She blinked. "What's sugar?"

"The secret of the dressing. Sugar. A teaspoon for every cup of olive oil." He chuckled. "And now that you know, I have to kill you."

"I have a better idea," she said, edging closer to him.

"What?" he asked suspiciously.

"You could seal my lips with a kiss."

His gaze slid from her eyes to her mouth, held there a long moment before returning to her eyes. "Lady, when this Ripper business is all over, you can count on that."


During the week that followed, about all Sara could really count on was Joe's edginess and the South Side Ripper's invisibility.

After that bogus article in the paper, the one that was supposed to shake things up so much, absolutely nothing happened. Not only were there no blatant attempts on Sara's life, there were no mysterious phone calls. No trash cans turning over in the middle of the night. No footprints in the snow. Nothing.

What there was, however, was nearly unbearable tension in the house on Westbury Boulevard. To Sara, it felt a little like living in a house with an unexploded grenade. Not that the human time bomb ever got close enough to her to cause any damage if he went off, though. And while Decker kept his distance, coiling tighter and tighter each day, Sara became more and more miserable. She took it personally. How could she not? She was sure his dark mood was because he resented being cooped up with her for so long. Who in his right mind wouldn't? Her sanctuary started feeling like a minefield.

It was time to do something, she decided by the end of the week. If the Ripper wasn't going to do anything, she certainly could, so after lunch one afternoon, without warning or ceremony, she handed Joe his leather jacket and his gym bag.

"Go home, Decker," she said, meeting his shocked, what-the-hell-is-this-all-about? stare. "This isn't working."

"What the hell do you mean, it isn't working? You're alive, aren't you?"

She tried to keep her tone level, matter-of-fact. "Yes, I am alive, but that's probably because the Ripper's a couple thousand miles away, stalking women in Alaska or somewhere. It's pretty obvious by now, isn't it?"

"Is it?" He cocked his head, regarding her intently. His voice was deep, gentle. "What's this about, Sara?"

What it was about was the fact that she was going crazy with wanting him, knowing all the while that he was going stir-crazy in her little world, that there was no happy medium for the two of them. Mr. Outside and Ms. Inside. Lieutenant Adventure and the wimpy little recluse. No matter how much they cared for each other, this just wasn't going to work. The sooner he was gone, she decided, the sooner she could get over him. As if she ever would. That was what this was about, and she should have told him that, but she didn't know how.

Instead, for a brief moment she was tempted to be cruel, to tell him she was sick of cooking for two, to demand that he begin paying rent if he intended to stay here in her house, to tell him to go back to his own place and rot there. Which, of course, was what he had been doing for the last three years. Oh, God. The mere thought brought a lump to her throat. She swallowed hard to dislodge it.

"I'm grateful that you've been here to protect me, Joe," she said at last. "I really am. But I just don't think it's necessary anymore."

"*You* don't think it's necessary," he repeated a bit belligerently.

"No, I don't." She narrowed her eyes and crossed her arms for emphasis. "And if you're honest, I think you'd have to agree that you've become a little obsessive about the Ripper."

"Obsessive?" The word nearly choked him. "Well, you'd know about that, I guess," he snarled.

Sara sighed, dropping her gaze to the gym bag. "I just think it's time for you to go. And, anyway, I just really want to be alone. Truly alone. You know?"

He looked bewildered for a second, but only for a second before his eyes took on a gunmetal cast and a little muscle jerked in his cheek. For a moment Sara thought he was angry, so angry that he was going to grab her by the shoulders and shake her until her teeth rattled like loose change. But he didn't. He merely shrugged, and then his scowl reversed itself to one of those lethal grins.

"Hey, no big deal. You're entitled," he said. "And you're absolutely right, Campbell. Our guy probably has taken a powder, otherwise he would've made some kind of move after that newspaper thing. Right?"

"I'm sure of it," Sara said, nodding.

"Yeah. Damn straight." He dropped the gym bag in order to jab his arms into the sleeves of his jacket, then he picked the bag up. "Well, you've got all my numbers, right? Precinct? Pager? Home?"

She nodded again.

"It wouldn't take me more than a few minutes to get here. If anything happened, I mean. Which it won't."

"I'll be fine."

"I wouldn't go, babe, unless I thought so." He juggled the canvas bag for an awkward moment, then lifted a hand to her face. The tip of his thumb trailed down her cheek while his eyes fastened on hers. "You let me know when you've had enough of alone, huh?"

*Now,* Sara screamed inside. Oh, God, why was she kicking him out when all she wanted was for him to stay? And why did he have to be so damned agreeable all of a sudden? Why did he seem so blessedly relieved to be going? Where was the Ripper now that she needed him?

"Sure," she said, trying to sound breezy and brave in spite of her self-inflicted wound. "I'll give you a call."

"Okay." He leaned forward, kissed the tip of her nose, then walked out the door without looking back.

And he didn't even caution her to lock up after he was gone. He was just gone.

Joe went home to shower and change after he was summarily dispatched from the big house on Westbury Boulevard. Home! What a joke. The place looked worse than ever. He'd been in shelters down on Russell Avenue that didn't smell half as bad. It didn't matter all that much, though, since he was going to be living in his car for the foreseeable future.

He stood in the shower, head bent under a hard,

pummeling spray, until the hot water ran out and a torrent of ice cubes forced him out of the mildewy stall. He nearly rubbed off a layer of skin when he toweled off, muttering into the steamed-up mirror over the sink all the while.

Obsessive. He was just doing his job, dammit. Or had been trying to do it until Sara had kicked him out all of a sudden. Here's your hat, Decker. Hit the street. I vant to be alone. He swore at his foggy reflection in the mirror.

He'd left her alone, hadn't he? He hadn't so much as touched her in days, and he had the raw nerves and the constant ache in his groin to prove it. That's what he got for mixing business with pleasure, he told himself. The booby prize for getting involved with a nutcase who'd let him into her cozy little world for a while, just long enough to make him want to stay forever, and then dismissed him. Just like that. He snapped his fingers, dropped the damp towel on the floor and went in search of a clean pair of jeans and a shirt with a socially acceptable amount of wrinkles.

His quest was a failure, apparently, because the first thing Maggie said to him twenty minutes later when he stalked to her desk in the squad room was, "Been sleeping in your clothes, Decker?"

He didn't even dignify her question with an answer. "Where is everybody?" he asked, slinging himself into a chair at an unoccupied desk.

"Well, let's see. Hammerman's out sick with the flu. The Geriatric Squad is checking out that new restaurant on Culpepper Street. Hmm." She tapped a pencil against her pursed lips. "Oh. And Cobble's getting a haircut prior to his press conference at five."

"Figures," Joe snarled.

"Yeah. Good thing the bad guys are slacking off this week, huh?" She grinned. "And speaking of bad guys, you see any signs of the Ripper over on Westbury?"

He shook his head. "Not a thing. It just doesn't figure, Mag. It's like the guy just disappeared into thin air after that Cormack piece."

"Maybe he did."

"That's what Sara thinks."

"But you don't?"

"I don't know what I think anymore." The springs of the chair squeaked when he leaned back. "But he's not gone. I can still smell him. I can feel him out there, waiting."

"For her?"

Joe closed his eyes. Sara was there in his brain with her tousled red hair, her deep green eyes, her lush Chocolate Silk mouth, so unyielding the last time he'd seen it. "Yeah. For her."

"I don't want to pry, Decker, but..."

"Then don't." He hauled himself to his feet. "I'll be in my car for the next couple of days. Beep me or call me on my cell phone if anything comes up, okay?"

"Okay."

He was almost through the door that led to the hall when Maggie called, "Bundle up, partner. It's cold out there."

He gave her a grin and a thumbs-up, even though he knew damn well she wasn't referring to the weather.

At five o'clock Sara stood in the kitchen, idly dipping a spoon in the sugar bowl, trying to remember whether Joe had said one teaspoon of sugar or one tablespoon for every cup of olive oil. She had decided to fix herself a Mama Savona salad, not because she was hungry, but because she needed the distraction. She wondered if it had been such a good idea, trying to make the salad dressing that had come to Joe by way of marriage. Maybe if she used a plain old bottled Italian she'd stop thinking about him.

He'd be here right now, she reminded herself, if she hadn't chased him away a few hours ago. Or maybe not. Maybe she'd just given him permission to do what he'd been dying to do all week. To fly the coop. To cut and run like hell from her claustrophobic little world. Who could blame him? If she didn't suffer panic attacks out in the real world, she'd make her own escape.

"Damn," she muttered as she dug the spoon into the sugar bowl, then shook off the excess to make a level teaspoon or so. She was about to sprinkle it into the cup of olive oil she'd already measured when there was a resounding *whump* in the vicinity of the back porch. The spoon flew out of her hand, and the sugar came down on her head like fine sleet. Ignoring the sugar fall and her thudding heart, Sara stared at the back door. Had she thrown the dead bolt after Joe left?

Yes! The brass knob was vertical. Locked tight. Thank God. Made braver by the sight of that, Sara edged toward the window and inched the curtain back. She gave an audible sigh of relief when she saw the huge mound of snow and broken icicles that hadn't been there earlier in the day. For some perverse reason and in direct contrast to her mood, the sun had come out that afternoon. She realized it had melted some of the snow on her roof, causing the little avalanche that had frightened her so badly.

Sara shook her head, disgusted with herself, determined not to let every little noise turn her into a basket case. The furnace was going to do that weird *pfumph* in the middle of the night, and she was going to ignore it. The refrigerator would do that *tick-tick-katick* that it tended to do occasionally. She'd simply turn a deaf ear. Those things hadn't bothered her in the past. They hadn't bothered her when Joe was here, and by God they weren't going to bother her now.

Anyway, the Ripper was long gone. She was sure of that. Even more sure since Joe seemed to believe it, too. He'd signed off as her bodyguard, after all.

"You'll have to guard your own damn body now," she muttered, grabbing a damp sponge to wipe up the spilled sugar. "You're good at that," she said as she dragged the sponge over the counter. "You sure guarded it from Decker, you stupid jerk."

She slammed the dirty sponge into the sink, turned on her heel—grinding more spilled sugar into the floor—and rushed out of the kitchen before her sobs could bounce back at her off the cold tiles.

Joe had been parked on Westbury Boulevard since four o'clock. It was six now. Time to start the car, blast the heater for a few minutes to warm up the interior against the dropping temperatures outside. Time to pour himself one more cup of coffee from the thermos stashed in the back. Time to bang his head on the steering wheel and call himself a jerk for being out here on the street instead of inside the big house whose lights cast a rich, golden glow across the snow in the front yard.

He had parked at the far edge of the property, close enough to let him see everything he needed to, far enough to be out of Sara's line of sight if she peered out one of the front windows. He didn't want to frighten her by letting her see he was still anticipating an appearance from the Ripper, and God forbid she should spy him and feel he was intruding on her precious privacy.

So she wanted to be alone. Fine. Great. He snapped off the ignition and shoved himself down in the seat, thrusting his hands under his armpits to keep them from freezing. Alone was good. You didn't have to deal with anybody's problems but your own. You ate when you wanted, slept when you wanted, left your clothes where they fell on the floor and strolled buck naked to the refrigerator any time you damn well pleased. Alone was fabulous. He ought to know.

Westbound traffic was slowing, most of the downtown drudges already home on a Friday night, making plans for the weekend. His mother had called him an hour ago to invite him for pot roast. "Bring that nice Sara, too," she'd said, trying to disguise a trill of hope in her voice, then trying not to sound disappointed when he said he wasn't seeing that nice Sara anymore.

His heart squeezed tight at the thought of not seeing her, really seeing her, again. At the same time, the thought of his mother's pot roast made his stomach growl. As many stakeouts as he'd done over the years, you'd think he'd remember to bring an adequate stash of food. The candy bar he'd eaten an hour before just wasn't doing it.

He picked up his cell phone and punched in the number of Dominick's, fully expecting Theresa to answer in that smoky voice of hers and to ask him, "You want the usual, Lieutenant? Large, thin crust, triple cheese and pepperoni?" Except it wasn't Theresa's sexy alto on the other end of the line, but the scratchy half tenor, half baritone of a kid, who went on to inform him there was no such thing as triple cheese.

"Put Dominick on," Joe demanded.

After he'd solved the cheese debate, the owner put the kid back on the phone for delivery instructions.

"Fifty-seven hundred Westbury," Joe told him. "But don't take it to the door. I'm in a car out on the street."

"You're kidding, right?" the kid said.

"Do I sound like I'm kidding?"

Apparently he did, because the kid hung up on him. Joe was about to call back when the front door of Sara's house opened, and he caught a glimpse of her in the porch light. He slid down in the seat as she poked her head out, looked up and down the street, then stepped outside, clutching a huge white terry robe around her. There was a white towel wrapped turban style on her head, a red scarf wound around her neck, and big, goofy red boots on her feet. She looked like an escapee from a North Pole booby hatch.

It didn't take Joe more than a second to figure out that she was sneaking out for the newspaper at the end of her driveway now that most of the traffic had dissipated. It also didn't take him more than a second to realize she had pulled the front door closed behind her to keep out the cold. Nice going, Campbell, he thought. Unless you're carrying your keys, babe, you just locked yourself out of your house.

She tiptoed along the sidewalk in those big, dopey boots, then followed his old tire tracks down the drive to where the paper had been tossed onto a bank of plowed snow. Paper secured under her arm, she started toward the house. Joe sat there, scrunched down in the seat, debating whether to summon a nearby squad car to help her get back in the house or to pick her lock himself and then have to endure another goodbye.

Well, hell. People had said worse things to him than goodbye. He jerked open the glove compartment, retrieved his case of lock picks, then got out and slammed the car door hard. The sound echoed in the cold evening air. Sara turned. Her white terry turban wobbled precariously, and when she raised her arm to steady it, the paper dropped to the ground. She ignored it, staring in the direction of the street.

He had parked out of range of the streetlight so he knew she couldn't see him. When his footsteps crunched across the lawn, coming toward her, she stood absolutely still and called out, "Who is it? Who's there?"

Idiot. What did she plan to do if it was the Ripper? Beat him to death with her newspaper? Snap her towel at him till he cried uncle?

"It's me, babe," he said.

"Joe?"

"Yep." Go ahead. Hit me with that alone business again. Tell me to get lost.

"Oh, Joe! I'm so happy you came back."

He just stood there, amazed, even a little stupified, while she galumphed toward him through a foot of snow, one hand stabilizing her floppy turban, one hand trying to hold together the edges of her robe.

"Joe!"

He opened his arms and caught her, deciding then and there it would have to be just this cold in hell— colder—before he'd ever let her go.

# Chapter 11

Sara stood behind Joe, hopping from one foot to another in order to keep warm while he picked the lock.

"I don't understand how that happened," she said, trying to keep her teeth from chattering. "I always keep the lock set so it won't do that."

"I changed it." Joe was kneeling, inserting a thin piece of metal into the keyhole, jiggling it. "I didn't want you to close the door and forget to lock it."

"Fat chance. So this is your fault, then, Decker." She gave his shoulder a little nudge with her knee. "It's a good thing you just happened to be passing by."

"Uh-huh." He was trying a different pick, patiently playing it in the lock.

"I guess I owe you now," Sara went on. "Dinner, at least. What do you think?"

"At least."

She was probably babbling too much, Sara thought,

but she couldn't help it. She didn't think she'd ever been so glad to see anyone in her whole life, and amazingly, Joe had seemed glad to see her, too. He didn't even seem to notice that she looked like a nightmare in white terry and red vinyl boots. Or he did notice, but merely believed her current couture was perfectly normal for a nutcase.

Well, maybe it was. Anyway, he was back and Sara had no intention of kicking him out again, no matter how tense or restless he became. If he left, it would be his decision, not hers. As far as she was concerned, he could stay forever.

He gave a quick twist to the little metal shaft he'd stuck in the lock. There was a distinct click. He stood up, turned the knob and opened the door.

"After you, Frosty," he said, stepping aside to let her pass into the welcome warmth of the foyer.

No sooner did Sara hear the dead bolt slide closed behind her than she felt Joe's arms encircling her, his cold cheek pressing against the side of her face, his chin nestling deep into the collar of her robe. "Alone's no good, Sara," he whispered roughly at her ear. "Not for me, anyway. Not anymore."

"I know. I missed you, Joe. The minute you were gone, I missed you. But I—"

"But nothing."

He turned her toward him, tipping her face up with a thumb to her chin, looking so deeply into her eyes that she imagined he was studying her very soul. If ever a man looked as if he had the words "I love you" poised on his lips, it was Joe Decker right then. Sara's heart did a swan dive into her stomach at the precise moment the towel on her head unfurled and flopped over her face.

Joe laughed softly, lifting the white terry slowly, dramatically, as if it were a wedding veil. ''Sara,'' he whispered against her lips.

The kiss that began with slow warmth—a taste here, a nibble there—didn't take long to reach searing proportions, especially when Joe's hand slipped the loose knot of her sash, then slid inside her robe. A tiny groan broke in his throat when his fingertips found bare flesh, and then it was Sara who was groaning when those fingertips performed incredible magic on her.

They were like teenagers, the two of them, loath to say good-night, standing in the foyer and greedily reaching for each other through terry and nylon and leather and flannel and denim.

''Too many clothes,'' Joe muttered after a minute, letting her go just long enough to peel off his jacket, then drawing her against his solid warmth.

''Let's go upstairs,'' Sara said, nearly shocking herself with her sudden boldness and the note of breathless urgency in her voice, wondering if her watery knees and melting bones could attempt the climb up the long marble staircase now.

Joe lifted his head from the fierce kiss in progress. He was breathing hard. It seemed to take a minute for his glazed eyes to fully focus on her face. His voice was as scratchy as his jaw. ''I, uh, wasn't anticipating this.''

''What do you mean?'' *Don't stop,* she wanted to shriek. *Don't stop now.*

A woeful little grin flicked across his mouth. ''I haven't carried protection in my wallet since I was eighteen, babe. We're sandbagged. At least temporarily.''

Oh, Lord. She'd been so consumed by the sheer heat

of him and by her burning need that she hadn't even given a thought to that. It had been so long since she'd made love that she'd forgotten....

And then she remembered the stash of little square packets her former fiancé had left behind in the bathroom drawer when he'd walked out of her life. But that had been over a year ago. Maybe they were expired. Or weird. Or the wrong size. Did they come in sizes? Was it rude to offer one man another man's condoms?

Her brain, already spinning from Joe's kisses, felt as if it were short-circuiting. She stared at him, blinking stupidly.

"I've got an idea," Joe said.

Oh, good! "What?" she asked hopefully.

He reached for the limp sash of her robe, looped the ends and tied a neat little bow at her waist. "Let's order a pizza."

Maybe at one time in his life he'd proclaimed that Dominick's triple cheese pizza was the next best thing to sex. Yeah. He probably had said that, but it had been when he was married and there actually were next best things to sex. Tonight, though, the pizza was a ploy, a way to buy time, a means to recover his control.

He paid the delivery kid, locked the front door and took the big flat box into the kitchen where Sara, dressed in something long and soft and black, was fixing a salad. Her color was still high. Joe attributed it to his kisses rather than the bitter cold outside.

"Dominick's," she said, spying the box. "I've never had their pizza."

"Next best thing to sex," Joe said, earning himself a withering glance while he planted himself at the island and flipped open the box. "Well, maybe not. But it's pretty good."

She served him a healthy portion of the salad. "Try it," she said. "I think I managed to get the dressing right."

Joe forked up a combination of lettuce, artichoke hearts and red onion, then chewed with his eyes closed.

"Well?" Sara asked.

"Almost."

"Almost? What did I do wrong?"

"You forgot the lemon juice."

"You didn't tell me about the lemon juice, Decker," she said without bothering to hide her exasperation.

"Didn't I?" He grinned. "Hey, I can't divulge all my secrets. I mean, we've only known each other two weeks."

"Lemon juice," she muttered. "So, what else are you holding out on me, hm? Oregano? Garlic?"

"Not this." He handed Sara a gooey triangle of the pizza, then tried not to watch her lips and her tongue as they sensuously tackled the melted strings of mozzarella and the thin circles of pepperoni. He sighed inaudibly. It was going to be a long night.

"Why'd you come back?" she asked, licking a bit of tomato sauce from her finger. "Was there some news about the Ripper?"

He shook his head. "No. No news. I just don't think he's flown the coop. Anyway, I guess I got used to guarding your body."

"It's a pretty quiet job." She shrugged, smiling a little wistfully. "All indoors. No traveling. No socializing to speak of."

"Great benefits, though." He took another bite of

pizza, letting his eyes roll back in his head while he chewed.

Sara sighed as she dropped a piece of uneaten crust in the box. "What I'm getting at, Decker..."

"I know what you're getting at, Campbell," he said, interrupting her with a stern, upraised hand, almost like a traffic cop. All he needed was a whistle to really get her attention. "It's not going to work, you know."

"What?"

"You're warning me off. Right? Trying to stiff-arm me the way you did this morning."

"No," she protested, then frowned and added a qualifying, "well..."

"Yeah. You are." He narrowed his gaze. "And I'm telling you right now it's not going to work."

"Why is that?"

"Because I've fallen for you. Hook, line and sinker." He snagged his mouth with his index finger, doing what he thought was a pretty good impression of a surrendering marlin, trying his best to make her laugh.

She did, but only for a moment. Then caution once again replaced the merriment in her eyes. "We're very different, Joe. Or haven't you noticed?"

"Oh, I've noticed." He let his gaze wander salaciously to her mouth, to her breasts, back to her mouth. She'd taste like pizza if he kissed her. Warm. Spicy. "*Vive la différence,* as they say."

"That isn't what I meant."

"You mean because I don't get all bent out of shape about the unknown, and you do."

"Well, yes," she said. "That's one way of putting it, I guess. Or how about your ability to go out and meet the world head-on while I just cower here behind closed doors.''

"Cower? You're cowering?" he asked teasingly. "Right now?"

She glared at him, strangling a little growl deep in her throat. "Will you please be serious," she demanded.

"I am serious, babe." He closed the pizza box, nudged it aside, then reached out for both of her hands. Clammy. Trembling slightly.

He wished right then he could just tuck her in his pocket and keep her warm and protected the rest of her life. He wanted to tell her that his life was composed of risk enough for the two of them and that if she never left home again, he wouldn't care because that meant she'd always be there for him. He wanted to let her know that he was sure she'd improve once she realized how much he loved her, how totally she could depend on him to keep her safe, to protect her from whatever demons she imagined were out there in the big bad world.

He wanted to say all that and more, but risk-taker that he was on the job, he was a coward now. Maybe it was too soon for such heartrending, gut-wrenching declarations. What if she didn't want his protection? What if she pulled away?

"I'm here for as long as you want me," he said. "Ripper or no Ripper."

The tension eased somewhat in her face, and her hands slipped deeper into his grasp. "I want you here for a long, long time," she said softly.

Apparently Joe meant what he said about staying because, once the pizza box was empty, he convinced

Sara to accompany him to his place for some clothes and other necessities.

It was still a pit.

"Why do I feel as if I'm rescuing a homeless man?" she asked only half in jest as she gazed around the wreckage of the living room.

"Probably because you are," Joe called from the bedroom. He appeared in the doorway, a yellow plastic laundry basket in his hands. "Not a moment too soon, either. I'm out of clean clothes."

"No problem. We can do them at my place."

He quirked an eyebrow. "We?"

"Well, I'll be glad you show you where the washer and dryer are, then you're on your own." She laughed. "No need setting any precedents."

While he gathered up a few more things, Sara began to regret her statement. She couldn't imagine anything nicer, really, than doing Joe's laundry. She glanced at the yellow basket, wondering if the bright scraps of fabric she saw were skivvies, imagining how they'd look on Joe's trim body. Anybody who looked that good in jeans would certainly look even better out of them.

"Ready?" he asked.

Sara nodded a bit guiltily, considering her thoughts and the warm rush of desire they inspired. She was ready, all right. Boy, was she ready!

Once they were back home, she slipped into pale pink satin, intent on driving Decker crazy if nothing else. She propped herself among the pillows on her bed, rearranged the covers and the pillows and herself at least half a dozen times, got up, brushed her hair, got back in bed, then waited. And waited.

From downstairs came the faint, rhythmic hum of

the washing machine, followed by the sound of the dryer. Finally, she thought, settling her shoulders a bit deeper into the pillows, encouraging one thin strap of her nightgown to slip down her arm, listening for footsteps on the stairs.

What she heard, though, was the washer starting up again. *Ka-chunga. Ka-chunga.*

*Ka-whoosh.*

''Rats,'' she muttered, abandoning her alluring pose and reaching for the TV remote on the nightstand. She punched her way through sixty-eight channels twice without finding a single thing to watch except the local news, so she turned the volume down and stared blankly at the snowflakes that dotted the weather map, hoping she didn't drift off to sleep before the Lunatic Laundryman finally called it quits and decided to wander up the stairs.

Joe checked the doors and windows before he went upstairs. He'd left his clothes neatly folded in the little laundry room, not knowing where to stash them. This moving-in business had been a pretty impulsive deal, and they hadn't gotten around to discussing sleeping arrangements. As much as he wanted to sleep with Sara, he'd already decided that, for the time being anyway, he'd better take the bedroom across the hall from hers. There was still the Ripper to consider, not to mention that pesky little problem of protection.

Not trusting the little stash of packets in Sara's bathroom drawer, he'd been tempted earlier to stop at a drug store somewhere between his place and hers, then decided he'd simply have to tough it out until there was no threat to interfere with their pleasure the first

time they made love. The last thing he wanted was for
the damn Ripper to catch him with his pants down.

By God, that was one son of a bitch he'd be happy
to see in the slammer. Forget that he had brutally murdered eight women. The guy was ruining Joe's sex life,
now that he finally had one again.

He paused on the stairs, listening to the night sounds
of the big, locked-down house, from the deep snoring
of the furnace in the basement to the drone of a news-
caster's voice somewhere in the vicinity of Sara's
room. He realized suddenly that he was hoping she'd
be asleep, allowing him to just sling himself out in a
nearby bedroom rather than have to confront his desire
for her all over again when there wasn't anything he
could do about it. The mere thought of that inviting
bed of hers was enough to give him a headache as he
climbed the rest of the stairs.

"Joe?" she called softly.

Damn. He stuck his head into her room, lit only by
the glow of the television screen. There she was, right
where he knew she'd be, looking all pale and pink, like
a little rosebud wrapped in tissue and washed by moon-
light. He swallowed hard, not daring to take another
step across the threshold. "I think I'll just crash in the
room across the hall, if that's okay with you."

He could tell from the slope of her mouth that it
wasn't okay. Already he'd learned to read her like a
favorite book or fairy tale. "The Princess and the Pea"
came to mind. Or "Sleeping Beauty." Some prince he
was, he thought. It wasn't the right time to make love,
but the least he could do was kiss her good-night.

"If you behave yourself," he said, stepping into the
room, "I'll tuck you in."

She smiled and slid a fallen satin strap onto her

shoulder. "I promise. I've never been much of a tempt-ress, anyway."

"Oh, you're tempting." He sat, edging a hip onto the mattress beside her. His gaze flickered toward the television across the room. "My boss had a press conference this afternoon. Have they shown any of it? I could use a few laughs."

"Not yet." She pressed the remote to turn the volume up a notch. "The local stuff will be on right after the commercial. Tape at eleven, as they say."

"Keep it on, will you? I want to see how he manages to tap-dance around the Ripper this time."

"Sure." She leaned against his shoulder. "Is your laundry all done?"

"Yep. And I threw in a load of towels, too. How's that for being domesticated?"

"You're going to be a pleasure to have around, Decker. You cook. You do laundry. What about windows?"

"Those, too. Just give me a squeegee and I turn into a maniac." He slapped the palm of his hand to his forehead. "Aw, hell. I forgot to check the windows in the kitchen."

"I haven't opened any today. I'm sure they're still locked."

"I better check them, anyway." He stood up. "Be right back. Give a shout if they show a clip from the press conference, okay?"

"I'll do better than that." She clicked a button on the remote. "I'll record what's left of the program for you."

"Good girl."

He kissed the top of her head, then left the room to trot downstairs. Who needed to work out at a gym when he had this museum-size staircase to keep him in shape? he wondered. He'd be glad when Sara dumped this white elephant and they could move into a little place of their own. Hell, he'd be more than happy to do windows if the inside view included Sara.

Slowing his trot to a walk, he told his brain to slow down, too. Maybe his heart was beyond recall, but that didn't mean he had to start making decisions that affected the rest of his life. There would be time for all that. Everything would fall naturally in place somehow after he brought down the Ripper, after Sara was no longer in danger. In the meantime, though, they would both be better off if he kept a clear and level head.

Just as Sara had suspected, the windows in the kitchen were all soundly secured. After checking them, Joe poured himself a glass of milk and drank it standing at the sink. Even that was nice. For the past three years, he'd been knocking himself out each night, dulling his senses with a couple fingers of bourbon. Even so, the morning's rumpled sheets were always proof of ragged, fitful sleep. What a mess he'd been. Until now.

He finished off the glass, then licked his lips, feeling a little bit like a battered tomcat that had finally come in from the cold. Maybe he would just climb into that big bed with Sara, nudge up against her pink satin warmth and purr all night long. Just purr, though. Nothing else. He swore.

Sara was still sitting up in bed when he entered her room. Her eyes were riveted on the TV screen, where Joe could see Frank Cobble holding court in a roomful of reporters.

"Turn the sound up, will you?" he asked, sitting next to her on the bed.

She didn't press the volume button. In fact, she

didn't move while she continued to stare at the screen. Her eyes were huge, as if she were watching a horror movie rather than the evening news.

"Sara?"

"That's him," she said.

"I know. That's why I wanted you to turn it up." Joe eased the remote from her hand and pressed the button until he could hear the captain's cigarette-roughened words. "Jerk," he muttered at the sight of Frank's neatly trimmed hair, custom suit and designer tie.

"That's him," Sara said again.

"My captain. Yeah. I told you he was—"

She clutched his arm. Hard. Her voice was high and tight. Terrified. "No. No. That's the face I saw under the ski mask, Joe. That's the South Side Ripper."

Joe laughed. He couldn't help it. The air rushed up from his chest and emerged as a distinct *Ha* at the mere thought of Fussy Frank in a dark ski mask, viciously gutting eight females.

"I'm not making this up, Joe," Sara insisted.

"No. I know you're not." He tried to wipe what he knew was an irritating grin off his face. "But I think you're confused. I mean, come on, Sara. That's my boss."

She took her eyes off the TV screen to glare at him. "I don't care if he's Santa Claus, Decker. That's the face I saw under the ski mask."

"Okay. Okay." He glanced at Cobble, who was winding up the press conference, having said nothing of substance for the past few minutes. "So the guy was middle-aged. Thinning light brown hair. A narrow nose. He looked like the captain."

"He didn't look like him," she said. "It *was* him."

"That's nuts!"

She ripped the covers back and bounded off the bed. "Well, thank you very much, Lieutenant. You and your people have been hounding me for two weeks to come up with some kind of description of the Ripper. And now I've done better than a description." She stabbed a finger toward the TV. "I've actually seen him again. Right there. And you don't believe me. Now I'm just a nut again."

"Sara," he said soothingly.

"Don't you 'Sara' me, bub. I know what I saw. I know *who* I saw. *Him!*"

"That just doesn't make any sense. It's—"

"Crazy?" Her fists lodged on her hips. "Go ahead. You can say it. I can see it in your eyes. They're all slitty and suspicious."

If his eyes were all slitty, Joe thought it was probably due more to Sara's thin satin gown than to anything else. Backlit by the TV the way she was, he could see just about everything underneath. The long, lithe shape of her legs. The sweet spot where they met. The jut of her hipbones just above. The soft indentation of her navel. He blinked to clear his vision as well as his head.

"I didn't say you were crazy," he said. "You're just wrong, that's all. If Frank's the Ripper, then I'm the tooth fairy. He's a cop, Sara, for God's sake."

"So? Does that mean he can't also be a killer?"

"Well, no, but…"

She was stomping back and forth at the foot of the bed, waving her arms, chewing her lower lip. "And here's another question for you. How come he's never been by here personally to talk to his star witness?"

"He was here," Joe said. "He just stayed in his car."

"Uh-huh. I guess he didn't want me to see him."

"That's ridiculous."

"Is it?" She stopped, her eyes widening, her mouth falling open slightly. "Joe, that's why the Ripper hasn't done anything this past week, ever since the article in the paper. Your captain knew all along that it was a hoax. That I couldn't identify him."

His eyes did get slitty and suspicious now. Not that he was even considering Frank as a suspect, but what Sara said made absolute sense. The Ripper should have done something. He should have made a move, some kind of move, on the witness who could put him away for life. It was inconceivable that he hadn't. Unless…unless maybe he did know that Cormack was just stringing him along with that piece in the paper.

"Maybe somebody tipped him off," he said, still reluctant to admit it. "It's possible, I guess."

"Possible," Sara said with a snort. "Maybe he didn't need to be tipped off. Maybe he knew from the beginning. Or when you told him what you'd done."

Joe thought back to that afternoon when the captain had sat in his car in Sara's driveway and blipped the siren to get Joe's attention. It hadn't struck him as particularly odd that Frank hadn't come to the door. The guy had been mad as hell, too furious to show that face to a civilian. It was his fury he had been hiding from Sara. Not his face. Wasn't it?

"What about the time you took me to the station for that lineup?" she asked. "Wasn't your captain supposed to be there and then didn't show up for some unaccountable reason? Huh? Why was that, Joe? Do you think maybe he didn't want me to see him? And what about—"

Joe held up his hand to silence her. He needed to think, but he couldn't while Sara was flapping around the bedroom, babbling at ninety miles an hour. When she opened her mouth to speak again, he silenced her with a gruff, "Be quiet."

It was like trying to put together the pieces of a warped puzzle. Nothing fit quite right. But still...

"Son of a bitch," he muttered, shaking his head.

"Do you believe me?" Sara asked almost breathlessly while she stared at him, studying his face. "You do believe me, don't you? You have to believe me, Joe."

He wasn't sure. How could he be sure? My God. It was too damned outlandish. Too twisted.

"Pack a bag," he said. "For a day or two."

"But..."

"Don't argue with me, Sara. Just do it. I'm getting you out of here. Now."

## *Chapter 12*

''Do not panic,'' Sara commanded her reflection in the bathroom mirror. Right. She might just as well have ordered the sun to come up in the west, she thought dismally. Already, her mouth was dry and her hands were wet and her heart was beating so hard she feared it might break a rib.

''Just ignore it,'' she told herself as she grabbed her mascara, dropped it into her cosmetics bag, then carried it to the open suitcase on her bed.

Joe was on the phone in the bedroom across the hall, presumably because he didn't want to frighten Sara with whatever gory details he was discussing with his partner. Every once in a while a not-so-muted expletive would drift in her direction, leading her to assume that Sergeant Maggie O'Connor was as skeptical as Joe had been at first. Who wouldn't be? she wondered. A witness who'd only been able to draw a blank thus far had suddenly drawn a detailed portrait of the Ripper, and he'd turned out to be none other than their captain.

Maybe she was wrong. Maybe her mind was playing some bizarre trick on her. Maybe she should just meander across the hall, laugh and say, "Just kidding," then come back and unpack this dratted suitcase. She wouldn't have to go anywhere, and her panic would subside. Maybe...

"You ready?" Joe's voice came from the doorway.

"No," she answered shakily. "Yes. I don't know. Maybe you ought to knock me out. You know. Just punch out my lights, put me in the trunk of your car and bring me to whenever we get where we're going."

"That's Plan B." He was standing directly behind her. His arms slid around her waist, and his cheek pressed against hers. "You'll be fine. You'll be safe. I promise. Jeez, baby. Your heart's beating like a jackhammer."

"Yeah, I know." She let out a long sigh. "What a wimp, huh?"

"I didn't say that." His arms tightened. "Actually, I think you're one very gutsy lady, if you want to know the truth. A lot of women would have fallen apart under similar circumstances, you know. With the Ripper and all."

"That's probably because I really didn't believe he existed until I saw that face awhile ago. You do believe me, don't you?"

He was silent a moment. When he did speak, his voice was more serious, more businesslike than usual. It was Decker's cop voice. "It's a real stretch, Sara. A real stretch. But Maggie and I are going to do some checking tonight. I've got to tell you, though, that both of us hope you're wrong. In the meantime we'll just keep you where nobody at the department knows. Just in case.''

"Let me just toss a few more things in my bag, and I'll be ready.''

"A few *more* things?'' He stepped away, then gestured to her brimming suitcase. "We're only going to a hotel for a night or two. You look like you're packing for a three-month cruise.''

"Humor me, Decker,'' she said. "And just be glad I'm not taking the kitchen sink, all right?''

He laughed. "Hey, if that would make this any easier for you, babe, I'd tear it out of the wall myself. I'll give you five more minutes, then we're out of here. With or without the sink.''

The lobby of the Jefferson Hotel was packed with conventioneers, but because of the late hour, the long, marble-fronted check-in counter was deserted when Joe and Sara arrived. He'd taken a circuitous route from her house, doubling back once to make sure nobody was following them.

He put her heavy suitcase down with a thud, fairly certain she had snuck in the kitchen sink and maybe even the bathtub while he wasn't looking. No wonder she never went anywhere. The packing alone was enough to wear anybody out, not to mention trying to maneuver the huge suitcase with its loose handle and wobbly wheels. He'd wound up carrying the sucker all the way from the third level of the parking garage.

Beside him, Sara looked pale and anxious, if not downright panicky. She seemed to be measuring her breathing, trying her best not to scream or take off toward the front door of the hotel. He looped an arm around her shoulder and drew her closer against him.

"We'll be upstairs in a jiffy," he said. If the damn clerk ever decided to show his face.

She swallowed audibly and leaned closer against him. "What if they don't have a room?"

"They *always* have a room. Trust me."

"It's awfully crowded." She gazed warily around at the conventioneers as if any one of them might suddenly decide to accost her, as if the Ripper himself might be lurking in their midst.

As if her nervousness were contagious, Joe found himself scanning face after face in the crowd, almost praying he didn't see a familiar one.

Sara leaned harder against him. "Joe, maybe we should just—"

"May I help you?"

The clerk had appeared on the other side of the counter, looking far more resentful than helpful. Joe was tempted to flash his badge in the guy's face to put him on notice, but he restrained himself. The less attention they attracted, the better off Sara would be.

"We'd like a room," he said, "for two nights."

The clerk frowned at a monitor while he punched several keys. "Looks like there's nothing avail— Oh, wait. No. Sorry. All I've got left is the Terrace Suite."

"We'll take it."

A decided smirk slid across the young man's lips. "That's six seventy-five a day, sir." His gaze flitted from Joe's worn leather jacket to Sara's pale, panic-stricken face, then back to Joe. "Plus tax."

"We'll take it." Asshole. Joe slapped a platinum credit card on the marble counter.

"Fine, Mr...." No longer smirking, the clerk read the card. "Mr. Savona. This will take only a minute or two."

After the man had turned and disappeared through a door, Sara nudged an elbow into Joe's side. "Mr. Savona?"

"My brother-in-law. I've got an extra card of his for emergencies."

She smiled a wobbly smile. "Like when you're stashing witnesses."

"Uh-huh."

The clerk emerged, paperwork in hand. He slid a pen across the counter. "If you'll just sign here, Mr. Savona, I'll have someone show you up to the suite."

Joe slashed his brother-in-law's name across the receipt, imagining the look on Rudy's face when he opened his bill next month, vowing to call him in advance so Edie's brother didn't have a coronary. "Just give me the key," he told the clerk. "We'll find it ourselves."

Then, with Sara's clammy hand in his right and her elephantine bag in his left, he hustled her across the lobby, wedging through shoulders and deflecting elbows, toward the bank of elevators on the north side.

"You're doing great," he told her as he hit the up arrow.

She offered him a tight-lipped smile in response, then didn't say a word as the elevator whisked them to the twentieth floor. The Terrace Suite turned out to be about half a mile down the corridor, which was good in Joe's opinion. They'd be harder to sneak up on. And the suite was adjacent to the fire stairs, which he devoutly hoped they'd never have to use in case of fire or anything else. He slid the plastic key in the lock, waited for the green light, then opened the door.

"After you, Mrs. Savona," he said.

He followed her in, wrestled the suitcase onto a rickety wooden rack, then took a look around the sitting room portion of the suite. Couch. Club chair. A desk too dainty to do any real work on. "Not much for nearly seven hundred bucks a night."

Sara had already wandered into the bedroom, so he did the same, spying the usual armoire to disguise the television, the ubiquitous double dresser and the bed. One. Huge. Round, for God's sake.

"Must be the honeymoon suite," Sara said, pointing at what looked like half an acre of beveled mirror overhead.

"Make you nervous?" he asked.

She laughed. "It makes me wish I'd lost those ten pounds I've been promising to lose for the past two years."

Joe sighed. "I hate to waste a good mirror, but I don't think we're going to be getting any sleep tonight. Maggie'll be here as soon as I call her with our room number."

"Maggie?"

"She's bringing the captain's desk calendar so we can compare dates with the Ripper's activities. But she has to have it back on Frank's desk before he comes in tomorrow morning, so we'll have to copy any pages that look promising."

"Do you think you'll find anything there?" she asked. "In a calendar that sits right out in the open like that?"

"I don't know, babe. But it's a place to start."

After Maggie arrived with the calendar, they ordered a pot of coffee from room service and divided the pages three ways, with Sara getting the months when the Ripper hadn't murdered anyone. This past year he had struck five times—twice in January, then in April, September and most recently in November, when he'd killed the woman in the Land Cruiser two weeks before.

By the time Sara was up to the second week of February, she felt she already had a handle on Frank Cobble's personality. He was cheap, obsessive, and he made more dentist appointments than anyone she'd ever known.

"This guy is really weird," she said, glancing up from one of the three-by-five pages filled with tiny, perfect letters, all of them printed in blue-black ink.

"No kidding," Joe and Maggie said in unison, both of them staring intently at their pages.

Like the detectives, Sara wasn't expecting to see anything quite as obvious as *Murder A Female* noted at midnight on any of her pages, but she hoped she might at least discover some kind of pattern in the captain's behavior.

"Who's Ellen?" she asked when she came across a note to order flowers on February twenty-fifth.

"Mrs. Cobble," Maggie told her, adding under her breath, "the poor thing."

"Who's F.J.?"

"Probably Frank Junior," Joe said. "I've got some notes here to write F.J.'s tuition check, buy F.J.'s airline ticket, stuff like that."

"Tuition?" Maggie clucked her tongue. "The guy's—what?—thirty and he's still in school?"

"Looks like it," Joe said. "You putting anything together, Mag?"

The sergeant shook her head, then sighed. "Not yet. You?"

"Nope."

Five hours and one more pot of coffee later, after checking, rechecking and cross-checking dates and data, none of them had come up with a single thing that linked Frank Cobble to any of the Ripper's crimes. The worst thing they had found was a reminder the captain had written on July nineteenth. *Reprimand Decker!!!* In the eleven months between January and November, those were the only exclamation points the man had penned.

It was almost six o'clock in the morning when, exhausted and bleary-eyed, they decided to call it quits.

Maggie carefully collated the calendar pages, making sure they were in order before she anchored them on their metal rings. "I'm out of here," she said. "I'll sneak this back on Cobble's desk. What do you want to do next, partner?"

Joe yawned, then stretched his arms over his head. "Sleep," he said. "Then maybe I'll go into the shop in a few hours and have a quiet little conversation with the boss. Maybe tell him that our witness finally came up with a solid ID and see if he twitches."

He walked Maggie to the door, the two of them with their heads together, whispering. Probably about her, Sara thought. Having the calendar come up empty hadn't done a lot for her confidence. Frank Cobble didn't come off as a vicious murderer on those pages, but rather a man who dotted all his *I*s, crossed all his *T*s, and sent his wife flowers for her birthday.

"Maybe I was wrong," she said after Joe closed and locked the door.

"Maybe."

He sounded as tired as he looked. His hair was rumpled from raking his fingers through it in frustration. His eyelids were at half-mast and his jaw was shaded with whiskers. Reaching for her hand, he said, "I don't even want to think about it anymore tonight. Today. Whatever the hell it is."

He led her into the bedroom, where he stood gazing forlornly at the huge round bed. "First time in my life I've been too tired to take advantage of a bed without corners."

"You've had a lot of experience in beds like these, Decker?" she asked.

"Well..." He shrugged. "Not exactly."

"How not exactly?"

He grinned, more of a sheep than a wolf. "Never. Dammit."

Sara whisked back the covers. "Good," she said decisively. "Let's just climb in, look up at that awful mirror and watch two sleepy people fall asleep."

They woke a little after nine, and while Joe showered and shaved, Sara ordered an enormous breakfast. Eggs. Pancakes. Bacon. Hash browns. Rye toast and whole wheat. Orange juice and coffee. If he was going into battle this morning, she didn't want him to go on an empty stomach.

But empty stomachs weren't what she was thinking about when he emerged from the bathroom wearing only a pair of unsnapped, half-zipped jeans that rode low on his hips. Her mind veered toward thoughts of flat stomachs, corrugated abs and powerhouse pecs. She reached for a glass of orange juice to moisten her dry mouth.

"How many people are you expecting for breakfast?" he asked, eyeing the linen-covered service cart with its array of dishes.

"I just didn't want you confronting the Ripper on an empty stomach."

He draped the towel around his neck, then picked up a plate and served a good-size portion of everything. "Here," he said, handing it to her.

Sara waved her hand. "No, thanks. I'm too nervous to eat. You go ahead." She poured herself a cup of coffee and joined him at the table by the window. Twenty stories below, traffic was moving at its usual morning crawl. Sara was glad she was far above it all. She sipped her coffee, then asked, "What do you think Captain Cobble will do when you broach the subject of my ID?"

"I think he'll laugh his ass off," he said, working his way through the pile of scrambled eggs and hash browns.

"Then you don't believe me." Her voice sounded more petulant than she had intended, but being a witness that nobody believed was turning out to be more than a little frustrating. It was infuriating, actually. She put her cup on the table with a thump. "Dammit, Decker. Why did you even bother to hide me away here if you don't think he's the Ripper?"

He spent a minute thoughtfully buttering a pancake, ignoring her as well as her question, then he shrugged. "I dunno." A little gleam shot through his gray eyes when he suggested, "The round bed?"

"Very funny."

"The mirror, then."

"Not funny, either." She slumped in her chair, crossing her arms and glaring at him while he polished off his breakfast, seemingly oblivious of her irritation.

"Are you going to be okay here by yourself while I'm gone?" he asked, picking up the empty plate and heading toward the service cart. "Cool, I mean? Calm? I know you'll be safe."

"Cool and calm?" she echoed. "Relatively. I suppose I'll just sit here and twiddle my thumbs while I wonder whether or not the captain puts you up in front of a firing squad *after* he laughs his ass off."

"I'm serious," he called from the bedroom, from where she could hear the sounds of dressing—the snap of jeans, the clink of a buckle being done, then the inevitable sound of a shoulder holster being tugged in place. "Sara?" he called.

"I'll be fine," she said.

"Because if you're worried or anxious, I can have Maggie come stay with you while I'm at the precinct this morning."

"No. That's okay."

"Okay." He was standing in the bedroom doorway, fiddling with his gun before sliding it into the holster under his arm. "I shouldn't be gone more than a couple of hours at the most."

Sara could feel her snit melting. She wasn't angry at Joe, after all. She was worried about him. It had been a long time since she'd worried about someone other than herself.

"Be careful," she said, rising to follow him to the door. "I mean, if I'm right..."

He looped both arms over her shoulders, bent his head to press his forehead against hers. "If you're right, I couldn't be confronting Cobble in a safer place, could I? Hmm?"

"No," she admitted. "I guess not."

"Keep the door locked and bolted while I'm gone. Don't let anybody in except Maggie or me. Not even housekeeping."

"All right."

"And one more thing," he said.

"What?"

"I love you, Sara Campbell."

Before she could do anything more than utter a startled little yelp, he had slipped out the door and pulled it closed behind him.

Frank was late, which wasn't much of a surprise. What was a surprise, though, was Joe's unpremeditated declaration of love. A real shocker, that. While he sat at his desk waiting for the captain to arrive, he replayed that exit scene over and over in his head, worrying because Sara hadn't responded in kind. No "I love you, too, Decker." No chirpy little, "Oh, how wonderful!" Not even a smile. Just a startled widening of her eyes, coupled with a kind of strangling sound in her throat.

"Nice going, Romeo," he muttered under his breath, crumpling another page from a scratch pad and aiming it at the trash can beside a vacant desk nearby. He never missed with these paper shots. He always scored. But he might have just fouled out with Sara Campbell, he was afraid.

Maybe it was too soon for her. Maybe she needed more time. Hell, maybe given all the time in the world she still wouldn't fall in love with him. He wasn't, after all, in her league. Pearl Street, where he grew up, was more than mere miles from Westbury Boulevard. It might as well have been a different planet. And just because Sara had enjoyed his family, that didn't mean she wanted to be a part of it.

He lobbed another paper wad at the trash can but hit Detective Carl Jeffers, who happened to be passing his desk at that moment.

"Busy, Decker?" the detective asked as he bent to pick up the crumpled paper, then tossed it at Joe.

"Busy waiting for Cobble," Joe said. "Any idea when he's going to show up?"

Jeffers let out a little bark of a laugh. "Your guess is as good as mine, Decker. That guy keeps the weirdest hours of anybody I've ever worked for."

After the detective disappeared into one of the interrogation cubbyholes laughingly referred to as rooms, Joe pondered those weird hours of Cobble's. The irregular times he showed up for work or left for home didn't seem to jive with the obsessive nature of the man. Of course, it didn't make him a killer, either.

God, he hoped Sara was wrong, not so much for the captain's sake, but for the department's. They sure didn't need another scandal. And this one—if Frank indeed turned out to be the infamous South Side Ripper—would be a lulu. The mother...no, the great-grandmother of all scandals.

He sighed, checked the time again, then rolled his chair back another few feet to lengthen the distance to the trash can. He had crumpled up almost half the scratch pad and was scoring four out of five shots by the time the captain finally appeared in the doorway of the squad room. From there, Cobble did a quick scan of the occupied desks. His gaze skimmed over Joe, then came back and locked on him. Joe gave a small, slow, openhanded wave, designed to be a greeting as well as an irritant. Shake him up a little, he thought, then see what shakes out.

The captain stalked into his office, slamming the door behind him. Only seconds later, Joe rapped on the wavy glass. After a gruff, "Come in," he stepped inside.

"Got a second, Frank?" he asked.

The reply came in the form of a grunt, which Joe took for a yes. At this point, he didn't much care whether Frank said yes or no. He left the door slightly ajar on purpose, partly to vent the smoky air inside but mainly as a test to see how much privacy the captain required once he was confronted. No sooner had he sat down than Frank went on the offensive.

"I pulled up your records, Decker." He took a mean drag from his cigarette, then squinted through the smoke. "You've just about used up all your sick leave. Just how much longer do you intend to baby-sit the Campbell woman?"

"Not much longer."

It wasn't the answer the captain expected. He sat up a little straighter in his chair, his head angling curiously to one side. "What do you mean?"

"I mean she probably won't need protection after we arrest the Ripper."

"Obviously." He tapped the ash off the end of his cigarette, then adjusted the ashtray so it was perfectly parallel with the edge of the blotter. "So you're saying you have some new information that might lead—"

"To an arrest." Joe finished for him. "Yes."

Cobble did a double tap on the cigarette even though there was no new ash since the last time. He checked the alignment of the ashtray, nudged it an eighth of an inch with his thumb. "Are you going to share that information with the department, Decker, or is this going to be another one of your grandstand plays? I'll have you know, Lieutenant, I won't tolerate—"

"Sara Campbell came up with a solid ID." He paused, but didn't take his eyes off the man he was about to accuse. "She watched your press conference yesterday, Frank."

The man didn't appear to react at all except for a quick, lizardlike flick of his eyelids. That tiny but telltale movement was as good as a confession in Joe's book, and when Cobble stabbed out his cigarette, then rose abruptly from his chair and started toward him, Joe's every instinct told him to draw his gun. But the captain brushed past him, went to the door and closed it. He stood there a moment, his back to Joe, his head bent almost prayerfully. The question was just who was he praying for? And what? For a second Joe wished he had brought Maggie with him as a witness as well as backup.

When the captain resumed his seat at the desk, he looked like he had aged ten years in the space of a few minutes. His face had taken on an ashen hue, and his eyes seemed dull, bereft of hope or even the spark of life. Frank Cobble looked like a prisoner of war. Haggard and hopeless and utterly beaten.

"Dear God," he said, "I hoped it wouldn't come to this. I hoped..." His voice broke. "I prayed so hard. So hard."

"You want to tell me about it, Frank?"

"She said it was me? The Campbell woman saw the press conference and said it was me?"

"That's pretty much the way it happened."

"And she was absolutely certain?"

"Yeah. Absolutely. A hundred percent."

Cobble reached for his pack of Marlboros, extracted one with trembling fingers, then had trouble flicking his lighter. He swore harshly and tossed the unlit cigarette into the trash can. "It's not what you think,

Decker," he said. "Here. I want to show you something."

When the captain reached down to open a bottom drawer, Joe tensed again, shifting his upper body to allow better, quicker access to his gun. His index finger twitched instinctively. If Frank came up with a gun, they were both dead men.

Instead of a revolver, though, the captain produced a framed picture from the drawer. He leaned forward, handing it to Joe. "Take a look," he said.

Joe scanned the eight-by-ten photo, angling it a bit to avoid the glare of the fluorescent lights overhead. It was Cobble, probably twenty or twenty-five years ago, looking typically trim and buttoned-up in Marine Corps dress blues. "So?" Joe glanced up. Cobble was studying him while he was studying the portrait. "Semper fi, Frank? What's your point?"

"That's not me."

"Excuse me?"

"That's not me, Decker. It's my son. Frank Junior."

Joe stared at the photograph. The resemblance was amazing. Father and son were nearly identical. From forehead to chin, the same. The same thin nose with its slight right cant. The same mouth with the same prim, disdainful slant. It was as if Junior hadn't had a mother at all, but simply been cloned from Senior. Just a chip off the old block. A replica. The difference in their ages, which must have been two decades, barely registered. They could easily have been mistaken for twins.

"Jesus," Joe breathed. That's exactly what Sara had done.

From across the desktop, the captain's voice was low and grim. "I've suspected him for a while now. Since

the fifth victim. I kept telling myself it was coinciden-
tal, though. Even when I did a search of his room and
came up with a pair of ski masks.'' His voice dimin-
ished. ''One had bloodstains on it. Could have been
from shaving. A cut. A bloody nose.''

''Did you ask him?''

Cobble shook his head. ''I don't think I wanted to
know, to tell you the truth. I kept telling myself I was
wrong. It was all circumstantial. F.J. couldn't...
wouldn't...''

''Did you find any weapons, Frank?''

''No. Only kitchen knives were always coming up
missing, then suddenly reappearing in the wrong drawers or the wrong slots in the knife block. It got to be
a joke around the house.'' He laughed weakly. ''Pol-
tergeists, you know.''

Joe didn't know. Not about ghosts, and not about
being a father. Not like this. He had no idea how far
he might go to protect a living image—an imperfect
perfect copy—of himself.

''What about motive, Frank?'' he asked. ''Any
idea?''

''He hates me.'' Cobble's eyes glistened with tears.

''So, why didn't he just off you?''

One of the tears broke loose and tracked down the
side of his narrow nose. He didn't even bother to brush
it away. ''I'm not a shrink, Decker, but my guess
would be that he'd rather I did that myself.''

Joe let out a long breath. He didn't like Cobble, but
that didn't mean he couldn't imagine the kind of pain
the man must have suffered for the last year or the pain
that was awaiting him in the future.

''We need to bring him in,'' Joe said.

"Yes. All right. He's due home from the university tomorrow."

"Any chance he'll run?"

"No. No chance. I suspect he's coming home for a reason."

Joe suspected it, too. And the reason was probably Sara.

Well, so be it. Now he wouldn't have to mess around with circumstantial evidence, hidden ski masks, disappearing knives that may or may not yield blood types or DNA or even Sara's belated ID. No way was Frank Cobble Junior going to be out on bail for the next five or six months pending an investigation. No way was Joe going to spend all that time looking over Sara's shoulder, sleeping with one eye always open.

He was going to catch the bastard in the act, then put him away for good. Whether that meant behind bars or six feet underground, Joe didn't much care.

He already had an inkling of a plan, the scaffolding of a trap. All he needed was the bait.

# Chapter 13

Sara was sunk to her chin in a bubble bath when she heard the suite's door open and Joe call her name.

"In here," she yelled.

She hadn't expected him to return so soon. The bubble bath had been a way of killing time, a way of distracting herself from worries about what was happening at the police station. Since they'd probably be checking out as soon as Joe returned, it seemed a shame to waste the huge marble tub and the complimentary vial of aloe bath salts. The luxurious soak was also a way of distracting herself from those three little words that kept reverberating in her head.

Decker had said he loved her. He loved her! She'd been so stunned that she hadn't been able to tell him she loved him, too. Idiot. He probably already regretted his words. She'd soon find out, she guessed.

Turning her head, she caught a glimpse of herself in the smoked-glass mirror that framed the marble tub all the way to the ceiling. The humidity had corkscrewed her hair into a red frenzy of curls, making her look like a soggy Orphan Annie. To complete the resemblance, her mascara appeared to have melted, outlining her eyes with big, black circles. Oh, great.

Joe tapped on the door. "Are you decent?"

"Sort of."

"I've got some news. Can I come in?"

She slid farther down beneath the thick blanket of bubbles, then said, "I guess so. That is, if you aren't offended by the sight of really wet, bedraggled women with pruney fingers and toes."

"That's my favorite thing," he said, pushing the door open and stepping inside. He stood there a moment, just looking at her, while a grin that could only be called lecherous worked its way across his lips.

Lecherous and loving, sexy and sweet, all at once. He looked like a sheep disguised as a charming wolf. Sara's heart started to beat so fast she was surprised the water in the tub wasn't churning as a result. Or maybe it was. All she could look at was Joe as he unbuttoned the cuffs of his flannel shirt and slowly began to roll up his sleeves.

"You said you had news, Joe." Not that she cared just then who the South Side Ripper was. Captain Cobble. Captain Midnight. Captain Hook. It really didn't matter. All that mattered at this moment was *this moment.*

He knelt beside her, bracing his uncovered forearms on the edge of the tub. "Yeah, I've got news," he said while his gaze drifted lazily from her head to the tips of her toes just peeking out of the white foam, then returned to her face. "Good news and bad news. Which do you want to hear first?"

She made a small shrugging movement that set the bubbles in motion, lapping at the sides of the tub. "You choose."

"Okay." He nudged one flannel sleeve over his elbow, then reached into the water, his ropy arm disappearing under the suds as his hand discovered her leg. "The good news is that your ID was right on the button."

"Ah," she said, not so much from the satisfaction of being right as from the hand that was moving slowly, invisibly from her calf to her thigh. "So it *was* Captain Cobble?"

"Almost." His hand curved over her knee, fingertips testing the flesh of her inner thigh. "It's his son, Frank Junior. Turns out the guy's a dead ringer for his dad."

"Mm." "I told you so" would have been more appropriate, but with Joe's hand moving slowly up her leg and her heart knotted in her throat, Sara could barely breathe, much less manage any sort of pleased, self-congratulatory comment.

"The kid's been back at school these past two weeks," he said. "That explains why nothing's happened."

Something was happening. That incredible hand had moved up as far as it could go, coming to rest at the juncture of her legs, applying just the slightest pressure, sending dizzying currents of heat, piercing shafts of need all through her.

"He's coming home tomorrow," he said. "This should all be over by tomorrow night, babe."

"Mm. Good." That was good, wasn't it? Was *over* good? She couldn't keep her thoughts going in a straight direction. They kept trailing off with every subtle movement, every delicious shift of Joe's hand. She sighed huskily, tried to focus on his face, then asked, "What's the bad news?"

His mouth twitched with a grin as the color of his eyes darkened to gunmetal. "Bad news?" He leaned forward, his free arm reaching deep into the water to curve around her back and bring her close.

"There is no bad news," he whispered against her lips. "Not for us, babe."

The big round bed was a tangle of ivory satin sheets, with Joe and Sara lying at a precise twelve o'clock. His face was buried in the damp and fragrant crook of her neck. His pulse rate was slowly decelerating, and his body was decompressing, but Sara felt so good, so deliciously warm beneath him that he dreaded moving. He shifted his weight slightly.

"Too heavy?" he murmured.

She shook her head. "Just right."

There was something in her voice, a little lilt of amusement, that made him lift his head. She was smiling, less like a sated lover than a sleepy, cream-fed Cheshire cat.

"What?" he asked. "What are you smiling at?"

Her shuttered eyes opened a bit wider and she kept grinning while her gaze lofted overhead. "Nice buns."

Joe murmured a soft, self-deprecating curse, then dropped his head, nuzzling into her once more. He'd completely forgotten about the mirror. He'd forgotten about everything except Sara while they made love. There was only her damp skin and soap-scented hair. Her giving flesh. Her hands on him, exploring, teasing, tempting. Her lithe legs and the sweet heat between them building and building until he couldn't hold back anymore. Until neither one of them could hold back.

He flexed the muscles in his backside. A kind of wink. Sara giggled.

"Next time I get the bottom," he said.

"I'll flip you for it."

"Oh, yeah? Maybe I'll just flip *you*, Ms. Campbell, you shameless little voyeur." He scooped her up in his arms and with one quick twist of his body, she was sprawled on top of him.

"No fair, Decker." She laughed, dipping her head to kiss him.

"Nice buns," he said against her lips while he smoothed both hands over her backside, thoroughly enjoying the view as well as the small rumble of pleasure in Sara's throat.

Ah, God. He wished they didn't have to leave this honeymoon suite in a matter of hours to return to the real world with its rectangular, unreflected beds and its assorted dangers. Slowly, he splayed his fingers on her soft, pale flesh, bringing her even closer, hoping he'd never have to let her go.

Against his will, thoughts of the immediate future began to intrude upon the afterglow. Knowing what tomorrow was going to bring, Joe could already feel himself becoming edgy, his focus no longer trained solely on the loveliness of the naked body draped over his. He knew he ought to get a solid six hours of sleep at the very least to be at his best when he tangled with the Ripper.

He angled his arm over Sara's shoulder to check the glowing dial of his watch. It was a little after five-thirty. Not much time left. But enough. As for Sara, he already knew he could never get enough of her.

They ate dinner in bed, sitting cross-legged and swaddled in the hotel's soft, one-size-fits-all white terry robes. Joe had ordered a bottle of champagne to toast their maiden voyage, as he called it.

Sara laughed as they clinked glasses, then, just as she was taking a sip of the cold liquid, a little chill that had nothing to do with the temperature of the champagne raced down her spine. The sense of foreboding must have registered on her face because Joe immediately asked her what was wrong.

"Nothing," she said, lifting her shoulders in a shrug. "Not really. It's just that when you mentioned maiden voyage, I started thinking about the *Titanic*. Let's hope ours doesn't end the same way."

"Can't," Joe said, taking another sip from his glass, grinning at her over the rim. "No icebergs around here."

Sara put her own glass down, then pulled her robe closer to ward off the sudden apprehensions. As opposed to her usual free-floating anxieties, these were based on very real dangers. "Tell me one more time how it's supposed to go tomorrow," she asked him.

"It'll go like clockwork, honey." He put a reassuring hand over hers. "I promise. You don't have to worry about a thing."

"Tell me anyway, Joe. I forgot what time you said Frank Junior's flight gets in."

"Four o'clock." He traded his champagne flute for a knife and fork, continuing to eat his filet mignon as if he hadn't a worry in the world.

Sara's world, on the other hand, seemed comprised of nothing but worries. Whole continents of them. "And then what happens?" she prompted.

"You don't need to know all this, Sara. All you have to do is—"

"I *want* to know," she said. "Otherwise I really will feel like a helpless worm skewered on a hook. If you're planning to use me to catch this guy, I want to know the details. I need to know."

He put his fork down. "Okay. This is the way it's going to shake out. Frank's picking his son up at the airport, then on their way home they'll shoot the breeze about what's happening at the university, what's going on in the department."

"Frank Senior and Junior have discussed the Ripper before?" she asked.

"Apparently. It's probably why the guy's been so successful for so long. He knows everything the police know. So Frank's going to confide in him that our heretofore unreliable witness…" He gave her a quick wink, adding, "That's you, babe," before he continued to outline the plan.

"Frank will tell him that your memory miraculously cleared and that you're set for working with a sketch artist first thing tomorrow morning. He'll also add, as casually as possible, that there's been a snafu in the department's scheduling and nobody's been assigned to you tonight. That unless he makes some calls, you'll be all alone in your big, big house."

Sara leaned forward. "And you're hoping that, while Senior is making those fake calls, Junior will show up at my house."

"That's the plan."

He spoke with such confidence, such ease, as if it had already been accomplished, as if it would work perfectly simply because mighty Joe Decker wanted it to. Sara, however, was more accustomed to seeking out the flies in the ointment, always anticipating the worst.

"Now tell me what can go wrong," she said.

"Nothing."

"Joe." She dragged his name out to two, almost three whiny syllables.

"Nothing is going to go wrong, Sara," he insisted. "Only Maggie and the captain are in on this so we can keep it as quiet as possible for the sake of the department. She'll be parked out on Westbury. I'll be in the house. Frank will be right behind Frank Junior. I don't expect the whole thing to take more than a few minutes once it goes down."

She raised a skeptical brow. "So, crazed killers always do exactly what you expect, Lieutenant?"

"In this case, yes." He put down his fork and reached for her hand. The corners of his mouth were suddenly weighted down with seriousness. Before he spoke, he pressed his lips warmly to the backs of her fingers. "You don't honestly believe I'd put you in any jeopardy, do you?"

"No, I don't. But it's not myself I'm worried about. It's you."

"Me!" He let out a surprised laugh. "I've been catching bad guys for a long time, babe, remember? Trust me, okay? Nobody's going to get hurt tomorrow. But, if anybody does, it's going to be Junior."

There was nothing smug in his tone, and nothing that even hinted at macho bragging. It was confidence, pure and simple. To the marrow of his bones, Joe Decker— the good guy—believed in his abilities. That confidence was evident in the set of his jaw, the firm line of his mouth and the unwavering gaze of his steel gray eyes.

"I do trust you." Sara sighed and squeezed his hand tighter. "And not only with my life. I trust you with my heart. I'm not sure I've ever done that before."

His oh-so-serious mouth gave way to the smallest of smiles. "That's because you know I'll take good care of it." The smile fairly sizzled when he added, "And all the rest of you, too."

As pleasing as the notion was to her, Sara winced ever so slightly. She moved herself up, then scuttled off the bed with more speed than grace before heading for the curtained window where she stood with her arms tightly wrapped around her. "You're not getting any bargain, Decker."

"I wasn't looking for a bargain, Campbell," he said behind her. "As a matter of fact, I wasn't looking for anything or anyone until you just kind of flopped down on the pavement right in front of me."

"No, what I mean is..."

"Shh."

Sara heard a rustle of sheets and then Joe was close behind her, his arms wrapping around her, his cheek pressing against hers and his warmth seeping through her back.

"I know exactly what you mean," he whispered huskily. "It doesn't matter. Honey, it doesn't make any difference to me if you want to stay cooped up at home twenty-four hours a day fifty-two weeks a year. It's okay." He brushed her cheek with his lips. "Hell, babe. It's great, even. It makes you easier to find."

"Well, that's one way of looking at it," she said with a pronounced sigh, still unconvinced despite the sincerity in his voice. She didn't doubt that he meant what he was saying. In fact, she was sure of that. He understood her agoraphobia. More important, he accepted it. At least he did now. But what about in six months? Being cooped up in the dead of winter in front of a cozy fire was one thing. What about in the good old summertime? How accepting would he be when June busted out all over?

"You don't believe me, do you?" he asked, slowly turning her in his arms until they were face-to-face. "Sara?" He urged her chin up with his thumb. "What do I have to do to make you see that I love you just the way you are and that I'm not going to try to change you? I'll help you if you want to change. I'll hold your hand or do whatever it takes, but only if it's what you want. What do I have to do to convince you?"

She bit her lip, blinking back tears, thinking there was nothing in the world he could do to make her believe there wouldn't come a day when he'd grow restless and bored, when all he wanted to do would be to break free of her limitations, to smash all her self-imposed barriers and well-constructed walls. "I...I don't think you can convince me."

He let out his breath in a long, exasperated sigh, but he never once diverted his eyes from hers or lessened the intensity of his gaze. His expression was somehow fierce and puzzled and patient all at the same time. "Do you even want me to try?" he asked.

"Do I—" The question took her completely by surprise. She had expected him to shout at her, to throw up his hands in frustration, perhaps even turn his back and walk away. After all, that's what everybody else did when she was being defensive. When she said, "Leave me alone," people generally did.

"Do you want me to convince you?" he asked.

"Well, I..." Sara stammered before she found her voice. "Yes. Yes, I do. Convince me, Decker, if you think you can."

"All right. Don't move," he told her. "Wait right here by the window."

Sara did as she was told, and while she stood there, she watched Joe move about their suite with deliberation, snapping off lights one by one, pitching her a grin from each lamp and wall switch. Finally, the only illumination that remained was the red dot that glowed on the smoke detector on the far wall. The suite was pitch black, and she couldn't see Joe anymore. What in heaven's name was he doing? She half expected that brilliant grin of his to materialize high overhead—disembodied, Cheshire-catlike.

"Don't move." His voice was just to her right, close even though she hadn't heard his footsteps.

"What in the world are you—"

Sara's question was cut off by a sudden whoosh of fabric. A distinct breeze tickled the back of her neck, and when she turned around, she found herself standing before a wide wall of glass, twenty stories above the night city and its moving traffic and myriad twinkling lights.

"There's your big, bad world, Sara," Joe whispered as his arms curved around her once more from behind.

"It's beautiful," she said, then added with a plaintive sigh, "from here."

He murmured in apparent agreement, moving closer, holding her tighter. "Look over there to the southeast. Right about at ten o'clock. What do you see?"

Imagining the cityscape below as a clock face, Sara decided ten o'clock must be where the big premiere light sat atop the magnificent old Nile Theater. At the moment, its long blue beam moved across the sky as if it were a glowing minute hand. "The Nile? Is that what you mean?"

"Uh-huh. Would you want to go there right now?"

"No." A tiny wing of fear fluttered in her chest, brushed against her ribs.

"Why not?" Joe asked softly.

"Too crowded," she said, trying to come up with a reason that didn't include the words *panic* or *attack*. "I just wouldn't."

"Neither would I," he said. "Want to know why?"

Sara nodded, feeling the day's growth of stubble on the cheek pressed against hers.

"I wouldn't want to go to the Nile because you're not there," he said. "Now, what do you see out there at, oh, about two o'clock?"

Sara gazed a little to the right. "In the park, you mean?"

"Can you see the roller coaster?"

She saw it clearly, outlined with thousands of multicolored blinking lights. "I used to ride on that when I was little. My parents had their chauffeur, Daniel, take me to the park a couple times a year."

"Want to go there now?"

"No," she responded immediately. "You know I don't, Joe."

"Well, neither do I. Want to know why?"

"Why?"

He moved even closer, as close as the terry of their two robes allowed. "Because you're not there, Sara." His lips brushed her ear, sending a scatter of goose bumps down her arms. There was a thread of amusement in his voice when he asked, "Am I making my point here? Or do you need more?"

"More," she said, leaning her head back against his shoulder, not sure whether she meant more touching or more convincing or both. Decker was so good at both of them.

"All right. Let's see. Aha. Just over there. Can you see the beacon on top of the Stolar Building?"

Sara's eyes had drifted closed, but she answered yes anyway. That beacon was a longtime landmark on the tall office building. It changed colors with the seasons, and she supposed it was either red or green this month, or maybe leftover orange from Halloween.

"There's a great little restaurant in the basement there," Joe continued. "Almost as good as Mama Savona's. Want to go?"

She rolled her head on his shoulder, meaning no, no way, absolutely not.

"Neither do I," he said. "Know why?"

Sara smiled. "Let me guess. Because I'm not there?"

"Bingo." His hand slipped between the lapels of her robe to gently cup her breast. His voice was like warm velvet at her ear, like the resonant purr of a barely tame yet deeply contented lion. "I want to be with you, Sara. I want to come home to you, wherever that might be, for the next forty or fifty years."

"Yes," she said. "I want that, too." She'd never wanted anything more.

Without another word, Joe scooped her into his arms and carried her to the bed where they made slow, sweet love. As if the next forty or fifty years were beginning then and there. As if they had all the time in the world.

As if their world that night was perfectly safe and secure, with no dark corners where danger might lurk. Just one big round bed. Population: two.

## Chapter 14

It was nearly one o'clock the next afternoon when Joe pulled into Sara's driveway and turned off the ignition. He'd move the car out of sight later, he decided. No sense in unsettling Sara with the tactical small stuff, plus he didn't want to jog a half mile along Westbury Boulevard carrying a not-so-easily concealed weapon.

"Home, sweet home," he said with a glance to his right, expecting to see relief on Sara's face. It was there, but it was accompanied by another emotion, one he couldn't readily identify. The slant of her lips was contemplative, almost sad. "What are you thinking?" he asked.

She sighed, looking even more wistful. "I was thinking that I'm really going to miss our lovely little sanctuary on the twentieth floor. I'm glad to be home, sure, but I loved being there with you. Every minute of it."

"Me, too." He curved his hand around her neck, drawing her close, then once again tasting the mouth that had become so familiar, so generous, so unbelievably soft and sweet. He had kissed her so much during the past twenty-four hours, it was a wonder her lips weren't calloused.

They had stayed in bed this morning, kissing and more, protected by the Do Not Disturb sign on the door, until nearly checkout time. They hadn't even bothered to order breakfast, because a visit from room service would have meant that one of them would have had to get up and get dressed, but mostly because they were only hungry for each other. Kissing Sara brought Joe's hunger back with a vengeance.

"We can go back there sometime," he said. "Anytime. Whenever you want."

"That would be nice."

Her tone didn't quite match her words, though, and when Joe pulled back, he noticed the tiny tic of worry at the edges of her smile. He could almost hear her pulse rate picking up speed, signaling distress. That served as a fairly emphatic if not grim reminder that their idyllic little honeymoon had come to an end, and it was time to get back to business. In Sara's case, that seemed to mean succumbing once more to her anxieties. In his case, it meant getting ready to bring down the South Side Ripper.

After he hauled Sara's enormous suitcase out of the trunk of his car, he leaned in to unlock the long metal box he'd had welded to the interior, removing his SR-60 sniper rifle with its night vision scope. Just in case Junior got a little unpredictable.

"Good Lord," Sara murmured when he emerged from the depths of the trunk with the weapon. She took a step back, blinked, then stared at him as if a black mamba snake had suddenly materialized in his hand rather than a black chrome gun. "You're not actually going to use that thing, are you?" she asked.

"What? This?" He grinned his damnedest, hoping to reassure her. "Nah. It's just a prop, babe, to make me look like the meanest kid on the block."

She shivered, obviously unconvinced. "I think I like your little gun better," she said, then shrugged and started up the sidewalk toward the house.

It had snowed while they'd been at the hotel, and as he followed her, he had to smile at the dainty little footprints she made. He'd have to remember to bring a shovel to clear the walk when he came out to move his car. Not that he really expected Junior to notice the size elevens that followed in her wake, but the more alone and vulnerable Miss Sara Campbell looked, the better.

It wasn't easy for Sara to pretend it was just a normal afternoon. After she unpacked—feeling foolish as she put away a ten-day wardrobe for their two-day stay at the hotel—she tried to work at her computer a while, but couldn't concentrate while visions of pistols and sniper rifles and ski masks reeled through her head.

She wandered downstairs and into the kitchen, where she tried to plan a menu for Thanksgiving dinner next week. She'd invite Joe's family, she decided. Parents, sisters, brothers, the entire crew. If she, Mohammed, couldn't go to the mountain, then she'd simply bring the mountain here to Westbury Boulevard for turkey and all the trimmings. But every time she looked at her watch or the clock above the refrigerator, she found herself counting off the minutes until four o'clock instead of calculating pounds of green beans and cranberries and yams.

Frank Junior's flight was due at four. Then Sara totaled up time for moving sidewalks and baggage carousels, a trek across a parking lot, a busy ticket booth, a long drive to the Cobbles' home and then the deadly trip from there to here, the trap on Westbury Boulevard. The mathematics of this cat-and-mouse game gave her a headache. She tried not to think at all, left the kitchen and settled in front of the fireplace, frowning into the flames while she punished her cuticles and chewed her nails.

Joe, meanwhile, seemed to handle the tension and the prospect of danger far better than she did. Well, he was used to it, she supposed. After all, it was his job. He spent the afternoon in constant motion—shoveling the sidewalk, driving his car around the block, doing a salvo of sit-ups and push-ups and just prowling around the house like a guard dog, eager to confront a burglar or two and to sink his incisors deep into a criminal's leg.

A little after four, Joe's prowling brought him into the den. Without a word, he kissed the top of Sara's head, then went to the phone, where he punched in a succession of numbers. Sara watched the taut lines of his body and the fierce concentration on his face as he listened to whatever was being said on the other end of the line. When he finally put the receiver in its cradle, he drew in a long, silent breath, then rolled his neck and shoulders slightly, as if to ease the accumulated tension there.

"The plane was on time," he said quietly. "It's at the gate right now."

"That's good," Sara answered, thinking it wasn't good at all. She'd much prefer to hear that Junior's flight had been canceled. Or, heaven help her, worse. "What if he doesn't come?"

"He'll come. Frank Cobble might not be the world's best cop, but he's a great salesman. He could probably sell snake oil to a cobra. He'll make Junior think that getting to you will be a cinch."

As if to emphasize his certainty, Joe pulled out his automatic, checked the clip, then returned it to his holster. Sara had watched him do that at least a dozen times in the past few hours. It was like a nervous tic. If he habitually inspected the rifle, too, she didn't know. He'd put that nasty-looking piece of equipment out of sight.

"I'll be glad when this is over," she said, rubbing her arms against a sudden chill, wondering how Joe coped day after day, year after year, with this terrible tension. It had to take a toll on him somehow. "We'll celebrate. I've got a bottle of Dom Pérignon I've been saving for a special occasion." She gave a mournful little laugh. "Of course, I didn't know the occasion was going to be the downfall of the South Side Ripper."

"Count on it, babe. We should have Junior printed and booked and stashed in a holding cell at the precinct by midnight, if not before. I'll tell you what. I'll put on my tux and take you out dancing. There's a—"

It was probably the look on her face that cut him off so abruptly. Sara could feel it herself—the way her mouth gaped and her eyes grew large. A fright mask. Tears began to puddle in her eyes.

Joe cursed softly. "I'm sorry, Sara. I wasn't even thinking." He sat beside her on the couch, drawing her into his arms. "Hey. We'll dress up and dance here while we get bombed out of our minds on champagne. Then we'll…"

She shook her head against his shoulder, the flannel of his shirt damp with her tears. "No, it's me who's the sorry one. This is just plain pitiful." She sniffed. "Maybe you should just shoot me and put us both out of our misery."

"I'm not miserable," he said with slow emphasis.

"Well, I am!" she wailed, hating herself for falling apart, especially with the Ripper practically at the door. The last thing this man needed was a weepy wuss on his hands. She jerked upright and began to swipe at her eyes just as the cell phone in Joe's shirt pocket let out a little chirp.

He pressed a finger to his lips, cautioning Sara to be silent, before he answered it with a brusque, "Decker," then listened patiently to whoever was on the other end of the call. When Sara raised a curious eyebrow, he covered the mouthpiece with his hand and whispered, "It's Cobble. Looks like we're right on schedule. He's doing a pretty good job of chewing my ass for not being able to baby-sit his prize witness tonight."

Until that moment, this whole plan had seemed unreal to her, but suddenly Sara, the prize witness, felt more like a prize wedge of cheese in a mousetrap. She sat back, letting her breath whoosh out audibly.

The conversation was short and mostly one-sided. Joe closed the phone and slipped it into his pocket. For a moment his expression seemed cold and inscrutable. Then one of those wonderful smiles careened across his lips. "I'd say we've got about an hour, babe. Why don't you go put that champagne on ice?"

Something was wrong, although Joe couldn't have said exactly what. After Sara had gone in search of their champagne, he put another log on the fire and eased out on the couch with his eyes closed, trying to puzzle it out. In spite of what he'd told Sara, plans usually didn't come together quite this well. There was always a hitch, a bump, a screwup somewhere.

Of course, he'd never worked a case where the perp was his captain's son, either. Damned if he understood why Frank had sat on his suspicions for as long as he had. Denial, maybe? An unwillingness to believe his own flesh and blood was responsible for so much spilled blood?

Since he wasn't a father himself, Joe couldn't pretend to understand all of Cobble's motives. But he knew his own father wouldn't have covered up for him one minute after a suspicion arose in his head. Hell, when his dad had found a six-pack of beer under his bed when he was fifteen, he had hauled Joe, and the six-pack, to the station house on Harris Street and left him there in the drunk tank overnight. Maybe Frank Senior had been letting Frank Junior off the hook all these years. Who knew?

The captain didn't want his son hurt, either. He'd made that absolutely clear. "You shoot him and I'll not only have your job, Decker, I'll have your head. Literally. If you kill him, I'll kill you. Is that clear?"

Cobble already had it all planned out. His son was going to plead guilty by reason of insanity. Then Frank was going to see that he received decent treatment at the state hospital. When Joe had wondered out loud whether Junior would go along with that, Frank had snapped, "He'll do what I tell him."

Maybe. Maybe not. Joe slipped his gun out of its holster and checked the clip one more time. It was a habit, a nervous twitch, whenever something like this was about to go down. Sara, he thought, hadn't exactly cornered the market on compulsiveness.

Sara. Just the thought of her made him want to touch her, so he hauled himself off the couch and followed the trail of her sensual perfume into the kitchen. It was almost five and getting dark outside, but she hadn't yet turned on the lights overhead. The only illumination came from the open refrigerator door where she was bent over, head and shoulders inside the appliance and her shapely backside poking out.

Joe's body reacted instantly and inappropriately, considering the time—not much—and place—a trap waiting to be sprung. He sighed, deciding he'd have to be content for the moment just leering at those luscious curves. But later…

She backed out of the refrigerator, straightened up, then gave a little gasp. "You startled me. I didn't hear you come in."

"You better stay on your toes, Campbell." He flipped on the overhead lights. "At least for the next few hours, because after that—" he grinned "—I can pretty much guarantee you you'll be on your back."

"Promises, promises, Decker," she said with a laugh. "Our champagne's chilling, by the way."

"Good. Did you remember to unlock the back door?"

She blinked. *"Unlock?"*

"Maybe I forgot to tell you," he said, heading around the island and toward the door. "No sense having Junior break it down. Besides, it controls the situation, knowing where he'll come in."

"Oh. Right. That makes sense." In contrast to her words, however, her expression said, *What? Are you crazy?*

"Come here," he said softly, opening his arms to her, then holding her close. "You're not going to be anywhere near here when it happens, Sara. That's already been worked out."

"What do you mean?" Her question was muffled in his shirtfront, warm against his chest.

"I mean Frank's going to give us a heads-up when Junior is a couple blocks away. He'll snoop around, see you at a window or two, then make his move. But when he comes in the back door, Maggie's taking you out the front door. You won't even be here for the grand finale."

"Why didn't you tell me that before?"

He smoothed his hand over her hair. "I didn't want you to have too much time to worry about it." He tipped her chin up, seeking the green depths of her eyes. "You would have, you know."

"Worry? Me?" She did her best to smile, but it was barely more than a thin, wavering line.

He kissed each sweet corner of it and would have gladly tasted the center if his phone hadn't started to ring, vibrating softly in his pocket between them.

"It's Maggie," he said, reading the ID window before answering with a brusque, "Yeah, Mag? What's up?"

"There's a problem," she told him. "Cobble's here. He wants you to come out so he doesn't have to explain it twice."

"What problem?" Joe asked. "What the hell's going on, Mag? Where's Junior?"

Maggie blew one of her irritated Irish sighs into the phone. "Will you just do what the boss wants for once in your life, Decker? I'm parked just up the street. Now come on.'' She clicked off, not bothering with good-bye.

He cursed, shoved the phone in his pocket, then cursed again. When Sara asked what the matter was, he was too steamed to answer. Instead, he stalked out of the kitchen in search of his jacket for Cobble's little meeting outside. A meeting, for God's sake. Outside in twenty-degree weather. He knew this had all been going too smoothly to be true. Leave it to a fussbudget like Frank to want a meeting just minutes short of the zero hour.

''I should have known,'' he muttered in the foyer, jamming his arms into the sleeves of his coat and re-positioning his shoulder holster, then ripping his fingers through his hair. He felt like a sprinter who'd just been warned to pull up short.

''Joe, what on earth is the matter?'' Sara had followed from the kitchen, close on his heels. She caught his arm. ''Where are you going? What's going on?''

''I don't know,'' he snapped. ''Cobble wants to talk to me. Maybe he's having second thoughts about taking down his son.''

''He wouldn't,'' she exclaimed. ''He couldn't. The Ripper has to be stopped.''

Joe's hand was on the big brass handle on the front door. ''I'll be right back. This isn't going to take long. Lock the door behind me, okay?''

''Okay. Hurry back.''

He stepped outside, pulled the door closed behind him, then turned his collar up against the bitter cold, cursing Frank Cobble with a steamy cloud of breath that turned amber in the porch light. It was dark. He could just make out the parking lights of Maggie's un-marked car half a block east on Westbury. She and the

captain were probably running the heater full blast
while they waited for him to trek the snowy distance
from the house.

"Hell of an idea, Frank," he muttered as he reached
into his breast pocket for his penlight, hoping its fragile
beam would at least keep him from slipping on a patch
of ice and breaking his neck. Rather than leave his
prints on the pristine lawn, Joe trotted down the shov-
eled sidewalk and driveway, then continued east along
the snow-packed sidewalk that bordered Westbury.

Headlights of passing traffic bounced off the front
and rear windows of Maggie's car, silhouetting her in
the driver's seat. There was no sign of Cobble in the
car, though. Joe cursed again. What now, dammit?
Back to Plan A?

Nearly at the car, he started to lose his footing on
the slippery sidewalk but shot out a hand just in time
to catch himself on the front fender. Finally, after a
few more treacherous steps, he reached for the handle
of the passenger door. Not only was it cold as dry ice,
it was locked. Joe rapped his knuckles on the passenger
window, hard, then tucked his freezing hands under his
armpits and moved from foot to foot while he waited
for Maggie to lean across the seat and open the door.

When she didn't, he called out irritably, "Come on,
Mag. It's freezing out here."

The door didn't open.

Great. He sighed a roiling, aggravated cloud of
breath. Locking each other out of the car had been a
running gag of theirs ever since they'd partnered up,
but what was funny in September and October wasn't
so damned funny now.

"Maggie." He tapped on the glass with the butt of

his penlight. "Maggie. Dammit. This isn't funny. Open up."

His fingers were so cold and stiff that he dropped the light when he attempted to turn it around. It plunked into the snowbank at the curb, then promptly went out, necessitating a minute or two of numb pawing before he found it again.

"I'll get you for this, Mag," he muttered as he shook the bulb to life, then aimed it into the car.

The first thing he thought was that Maggie had covered herself with a blanket because of the cold. It seemed to penetrate his brain slowly—by centimeters—by seconds that somehow felt like years—that the blanket was red, and it wasn't a blanket at all that covered her. His partner was covered with blood.

He jerked the beam of light to her throat. Jesus, Joseph and Mary. His vision blurred and his knees nearly buckled and it took all his will to keep from retching. And then, even before he knew he had turned around, Joe was staring at the brightly lit front door of Sara's house.

Locked. Yes, he knew that. He had heard her turn the bolt. But not the back door. Not the back. The back.

"Leave the back door open," Frank had said.

# Chapter 15

In the foyer, peeking out one of the frosted glass sidelights of the door, Sara couldn't see a thing except the vague, almost jewel-like impressions of headlights and taillights on Westbury. But she was almost certain she heard Joe call to her to lock the door, which made no sense at all because he'd been standing just outside on the porch a few minutes ago when she had locked it.

She was positive she had locked it. Just to reassure herself, though, she glanced at the brass knob of the dead bolt again. Sure enough, it was vertical. Locked up tight. So why in the world was he yelling at her to do it again?

Then, with a slap of her palm to her head, Sara answered her own silent question out loud. "The *back* door, you idiot. He wants you to lock the back door."

She whirled, raced down the long hallway and skidded barefoot into the dark kitchen. At the same moment she flipped on the lights, she seemed to recall not turning them off when she'd followed the grumbling, growling Decker out of the kitchen earlier. Maybe she had, though. It didn't matter, anyway. No sense worrying about lights when she was supposed to be worrying about locks. She gave a tiny shrug, then quickly advanced to the back door.

The floor was wet! Wet and cold. It felt like melted snow beneath her bare toes. Now how in the world…? Who…? Sara's gaze snapped to the door. Joe had unlocked it earlier. She knew that because she'd watched him do it. He'd practically made a federal case out of it. But now the door was locked. The dead bolt had been thrown. How could that be when she was the only one in the house?

A cold prickle of fear traveled from the top of her head down the length of her spine, and she stood there frozen for a moment, unable to move or to think, staring at the lock. Then, without a sound, the doorknob began to turn.

Sara screamed.

The knob jiggled furiously and Joe's voice sounded from the opposite side. ''Sara! It's me. Open the door. Hurry.''

No sooner had she turned the bolt than he was reaching in to grab her wrist and pull her onto the back porch.

''Joe! Oh, I've never been so glad to—''

He hushed her with a hand over her mouth. ''Listen to me. I lost my phone in the snow. Run to a neighbor's. Call nine-one-one and tell them an officer's down and another one needs assistance. Then stay there, Sara. Don't come back.'' He grasped her shoulders and gave her a little shake. ''You stay there. Do you hear me?''

She nodded, even though his words barely registered. Rather, it was the look on his face—fierce, warriorlike, lethal—that made her understand on a purely instinctive level that she had to do exactly what he told her. Only she didn't want to leave him. Ever. She was safe when she was with him. Something had gone terribly wrong and she wanted to help him.

"Joe, I..."

"Go," he ordered, whirling her around, pointing her toward the house next door, then giving her a push. "Now, Sara. Run."

She ran, her bare feet stinging in the snow, her teeth clenched against the bitter cold. Only once did she turn to look for Joe, but he wasn't there anymore. The back door was closed.

Joe doused the kitchen lights, allowing himself only a second to be blessedly relieved that Sara was safely out of the house and that she hadn't given him an argument when he'd practically tossed her out in the cold without much explanation. *That's my girl,* he thought, before he slipped cautiously into the dark hall that led to the foyer. His automatic tight in his grasp, he edged sideways with his back against the wall, trying to make himself as small a target as possible, fighting against the natural instinct to move fast when in pursuit.

Both sides of the long corridor were decked with framed artwork, he remembered, so he doubled his caution for fear of dislodging an etching or a lithograph and sending it crashing to the floor. He practically held his breath for the entire thirty feet. Then, just as he was nearing the hallway's end—where the carpeted floor gave way to marble—he was aware of a distinct change in temperature. In fact, all of a sudden, it felt damned cold. Almost as if...

He shoved off the wall, peered into the foyer, then swore out loud.

''Son of a bitch.''

The front door was open. Wide. Beyond the snowy expanse of lawn, he could see the passing traffic on Westbury. An icy breeze hit Joe almost like a slap across the face. The bastard wasn't in the house, after all. He had come in the unlocked back, hidden, probably waited until Joe sent Sara off, and then slipped out the front. To get Sara!

He swore again, then turned to retrace his steps down the dark hall, only faster. He had to get his rifle with the night scope. He'd stashed it in the little bathroom off the kitchen, knowing it made Sara nervous, thinking he'd never need it anyway because the plan was all supposed to go down in the house. Dammit. He should have figured that a twisted mind would turn the whole thing into a maze.

Almost running, his momentum carried him around the corner into the dark kitchen. Then there was only half a heartbeat to react to the lunging shadow and to deflect the angle of the blade.

Her neighbors, the Carsons, hadn't been home, and it had taken Sara far too many precious minutes to convince their non-English speaking maid that she had to use their phone. The emergency dispatcher had told her to stay calm and to stay on the line, but Sara couldn't do either. She hung up and started back to her own house, not knowing exactly what had gone wrong or what she was going to do about it but knowing she couldn't camp out next door while Joe was in trouble.

Other than the sound of her bare feet crunching in the snow, the night was eerily quiet.

She tilted her head, hoping to hear the sound of a distant siren, the flash of oncoming lights. Nothing. Oh, God. She should have done as the dispatcher told her, she thought. She should have stayed on the line. Maybe it was some sort of test. Maybe the nine-one-one people relegated all hang-ups to the crank file.

She stood there a moment, not knowing which way to go—back to the Carsons' to call for help again or on to her house to help Joe in any way she could. Back, she decided. She had to call again. She turned as fast as her frozen feet would permit, then the rest of her body froze.

From behind the ski mask, the Ripper's eyes glinted feverishly. More wolf than man. Sara tried to scream but the cold air rushed into her throat and shattered her cry like broken glass, like thin ice cracking over a black, bottomless pool.

Joe leaned heavily, bracing himself against the frame of the back door, willing himself to stay conscious, to stave off the shock that kept threatening to shut his system down. He didn't know how bad he was hurt, but he knew the knife was jammed in his side up to its hilt and that he didn't dare remove it for fear of bleeding to death. All he needed was a minute, maybe two, to get a clean shot.

All he needed was for Sara to hold still. Through the scope, in surreal monochromes, he watched her putting up the fight of her life, twisting and tugging and scratching at the arms that were dragging her relentlessly toward the trees at the rear of the yard. If she'd just quit struggling for a second, quit coming into the crosshairs...

"Hold still, babe," he whispered, barely getting the words past his chattering teeth. He leaned against the door frame, steadying himself. He bit his lower lip to sharpen what was left of his concentration.

Somewhere on Westbury, blocks away, Joe heard sirens begin to wail. Good. That was good. But they wouldn't be here soon enough.

Sara must've heard them, too. All of a sudden, she tilted her pretty head, lifted her chin and held still as if to listen.

Joe bit down harder on his lip and squeezed the trigger.

The Ripper toppled backward, taking Sara with him into the deep and snowy branches of a pine. Still clamped tightly in his arms, she thought he'd merely lost his balance or had dived for cover at the rifle's earsplitting crack. She lay there a moment, prone in the snow, feeling dazed and disoriented. But then, with a jolt, she realized that not only was her attacker not attacking her any longer, he wasn't even holding her. With a cry that was closer to a whimper, she scrambled from beneath the dead weight of his thick wool sleeves and through the heavy snow-laden boughs.

The sirens she had heard only a moment before changed their timbre as vehicle after vehicle came screeching to a halt in the drive. Lights—red and blue and hot white—pierced the darkness of the back yard and lit up the night. Doors opened and thumped closed. Suddenly men in uniforms were everywhere. A helicopter appeared over her rooftop, its blades thrashing the air and its beam streaking into every corner of the yard.

Somebody took her by the arm. "Are you all right, miss?"

She blinked at the young policeman, not knowing for a second what the correct answer was. She heard herself utter yes, even though what she meant was no. No, she wasn't all right. Where was Joe? Her frantic gaze swept what was nearly a crowd scene behind her house. "Where's Joe? Lieutenant Decker?"

"Decker?" The young man shrugged. "I don't know if he's even on duty tonight, miss." He called to one of the men surrounding the Ripper's fallen body. "Hamilton, you seen Joe Decker anywhere around here?"

The officer jerked a thumb over his shoulder. "Up there. Looks like he's in pretty bad shape. He took a knife in the gut."

"No." The word broke painfully in Sara's throat, and then, despite her bare feet and liquid knees and shaky legs, she started toward the house. "Joe!" She tried to call to him through the chaos on the ground and the hectic swirling of the chopper blades overhead. "Joe!"

"Sara!"

His hoarse cry cut through all the chaos and commotion. Sara stumbled and dropped to her knees, but the young policeman helped her up.

"Over here," he said. "This way, miss." He elbowed a uniformed man out of his way. "Coming through. Watch out for the lady here."

She saw him in one swoop of the helicopter's bright beam. He was sitting on the back porch steps, fending off a frantic pair of hands trying to attach an oxygen mask to his face. His beautiful, beautiful, pale and pain-racked face.

"Joe!" Sara ran as best she could until she reached him, until she could put out a hand and touch his knee, his arm, his cheek.

"Hey, babe." He drew in a breath. "You're okay. You're okay." He said it again and again.

He seemed to dredge deep inside himself to bring up a smile, then tipped his head into her hand, briefly touching his trembling lips to her palm. The relief in his eyes was deep and sweet, but Sara could see the relief was battling with pain. In spite of herself, she allowed her gaze to leave his face, to drop to the place where a wooden handle of a knife protruded from his shirt just above his belt. She stared in horror, then a firm arm nudged her away.

"We need room here, hon. You'll have to move back." The woman who spoke had tight, dark curls and coffee-colored skin. She wrapped a blood pressure cuff around Joe's arm and, while she pumped it up, she turned her head to Sara. "You're the Sara that the lieutenant keeps going on about?"

Sara nodded. "How...how is he?"

The paramedic was quiet for a moment, listening for Joe's pulse with her stethoscope. Other than a thinning of her lips, her expression gave nothing away.

"The knife," Sara whispered. "Can't you take it out?"

"We'll let them take care of that in the ER," she answered calmly. "We're going to move you onto the stretcher now, Lieutenant. Okay?"

Joe barely nodded in response. "Sara. Where's Sara?"

"Right here, Joe." Sara leaned as close as she could. "I'm right here with you. You're going to be fine."

A ghost of a grin played at the edges of his mouth, but his lips barely moved when he said, "This knife. I feel like a piece of steak."

"And now you're about to feel like a pincushion, Lieutenant, 'cause I've gotta start a line now," the paramedic said as she took his hand and deftly inserted a needle into a vein, then taped it down.

He closed his eyes a moment as if gathering strength to speak. "You're all right, Sara? Did Cobble hurt you?"

"No, he didn't hurt me. I'm fine except for a few broken nails. I can't say the same for Junior, though."

"Not Junior, honey. It was Frank Senior."

Sara's mouth fell open.

Joe swore softly, weakly. "He suckered me in real good, the son of a bitch. I'm sorry, babe." His eyes, already glassy, flooded with tears. "Jesus. I thought I was going to lose you."

A lump lodged in her throat, but somehow she managed to let out a little laugh. "Lose me! I don't think so, Decker. Weren't you the guy who said he liked my agoraphobia because it makes me easy to find?"

He blinked a slow, wet and maybe even grateful yes.

"So you're never going to lose me," Sara continued. "I'll always be right here."

"Lock your doors, Campbell, till…till I get back." He tried to grin and failed miserably.

Tears blurred Sara's eyes, but before she could respond, a firm hand gripped her elbow and pulled her up and aside. "No more talking now, hon," the paramedic said. "We gotta hustle. You can see him at Saint Cat's."

* * *

Joe was feeling better, probably because of whatever was dripping into him from the bag overhead while he waited for a CAT scan. At least he was feeling strong enough to countermand the doc's prohibition against visitors in his little curtained-off corner of the dingy ER at Saint Cat's. The only problem was that those visitors—Sig Tully, a detective from the fourth precinct, and Bob Tober of Internal Affairs—were having a hard time questioning him and at the same time keeping their eyes off the knife that was still sticking in Joe's gut. In fact, if Joe felt just a tad better, he really would have enjoyed Tober's pale, practically luminous shade of green.

No. That wasn't true. If he felt better, he'd be out somewhere tossing back one after another neat Scotches trying to forget that Maggie was dead and that Frank Cobble had murdered her. If Joe had been smarter, sharper, quicker, less gullible, more cautious, his partner might still be alive. And Sara. Dear God, he hardly dared think about her right now. He'd come so close to losing her. A matter of seconds. Mere inches.

"So, you're pretty sure Cobble's our guy for the other eight victims?" Tully asked him, breaking into his thoughts.

"Makes sense," Joe said.

The detective quirked an eyebrow. "And a motive? You got any ideas?"

"Hey, I'm not a shrink, Tully." He started to shrug, but after his shoulders had lifted less than half an inch, the knife protested by sending a white hot comet of pain across his abdomen. He cursed and clenched his teeth.

Tully and Tober exchanged looks.

"Well." Tober snapped his notebook closed. "We can go over this later. We'll let you get some rest now, Decker."

Before they could make a quick escape through the curtains, Joe asked, "Are you guys going back to question Sara Campbell now?"

"No," Tully said, turning back. "We did a preliminary on the way over here. That's enough for tonight. She's pretty shook up."

"Over here?" Joe thought he had misunderstood. He'd been about to ask the detective to make sure Sara's sanctuary on Westbury was secure after the events of the evening. "What do you mean?"

"I mean we questioned her when we were driving her over here."

Joe blinked. "Here? You mean Saint Cat's?"

"Yeah, Decker. Saint Cat's. She's out in the waiting room with your family."

The fact that his family was already here, probably packing the waiting room wall to wall, was no surprise. But Sara? Tully had said she was shook up, but the detective didn't know the half of it.

"See if you can sneak her back here, will you?" Joe asked him.

Tully gave him a thumbs-up, then disappeared. While he waited, Joe attempted to arrange the sheet that covered his legs so it partly concealed the knife handle. He was used to it now. The damn thing almost seemed like a natural part of him. But he didn't want to upset Sara more than she already was. He'd do his best to smooth her anxieties, then he'd ask his mother or one of his sisters to take her home and stay with her a while.

He saw her hand first with its broken fingernails as

she slipped the curtain back. His heart twisted, then promptly tied itself into a bow when her pretty face came into view.

"Hi," she said softly, approaching the table where he was propped up and sliding her hand into his. "I thought you were upstairs getting a CAT scan."

"I would be if this were Central Methodist or University Hospital. I think they decided the cardiac arrest down the hall takes precedence." He squeezed her hand. "I'm going to have somebody take you home."

Her green eyes got a little larger, and her mouth took a stubborn turn. "You are not. I'm not leaving until you leave, bub."

It was only then that he realized the hand curved in his wasn't clammy or trembling, but cool and calm and dry. "You're doing okay?" he asked. "I mean, really okay?" He tapped his chest with his other hand. "No pitty pats or anything? No hyperventilating? All that stuff?"

She didn't answer, but simply stared at him for a minute as if she hadn't quite understood what he'd said. Then, barely above a whisper, she said, "No. None of that."

He raised an eyebrow. "You're not in Kansas, you know, Dorothy. You're out in the big bad world." He gestured around the dismal little space. "And this is about as bad as it gets."

A tiny smile flickered across her mouth, and then he watched as her expression underwent a succession of mutations in an instant. Bewilderment. Amazement. Pleasure. Pride.

"I really *am* okay," she said, as if she had to voice it to fully believe it.

"You're more than okay, Campbell," he said, bringing her hand to his lips, kissing each ragged fingertip. "You're beautiful and you're brave and, lucky for me, you're all mine."

# *Epilogue*

The Deckers postponed Thanksgiving until Joe was released from the hospital and able to walk without grinding out oaths every few steps. He wasn't just lucky to have Sara. He was lucky the knife blade had skidded along a rib and hadn't turned toward his lung before it lodged in subcutaneous fat, even though he protested loudly that there wasn't an ounce of fat, subcutaneous or otherwise, on his body. He was healing fast, and Sara was looking forward to the day when his scar began to fade along with the horrible memories of the Ripper.

She was also looking forward to the Thanksgiving gathering of the clan at Rose and Mike Decker's house on Pearl Avenue. But she and Joe were running late because Sara had insisted on stopping at a convenience store along the way for enough eggnog to supply a small army.

Because of the holiday the little store was mobbed,

and when Joe saw the long checkout line through the window, he immediately offered to be the designated shopper.

"Not on your life, pal," Sara said. "I do lines now. Remember?"

And she had, without a palpitation or a single bead of cold sweat. She couldn't have explained why she was suddenly free of panic. Maybe it was because she'd experienced enough panic and anxiety to last a lifetime on that terrible night when Joe was stabbed. Or maybe it was because she was so in love with him that there wasn't room in her for any other emotion. Probably it was because, for the first time in her life, she felt truly loved and protected.

The little house on Pearl Avenue radiated welcome and good cheer behind its facade of Christmas lights. Mike, the oldest brother, met them at the door. He relieved her of her bags of eggnog, passed them to what appeared to be a bucket brigade that went all the way to the kitchen. Then he gave Sara a great bear hug, after which he embraced Joe almost delicately.

"How's my little bro?" he asked, his eyes moist and full of concern.

"Better every day," Joe told him. "Plus, I've got a scar to put your little motorcycle scratch to shame, big brother."

"No way," Mike said.

"Five bucks says mine's better." Joe waggled his brows. "Longer, too."

Sara rolled her eyes. "Oh, please."

"Longer, huh?" Mike grinned one of those killer grins that apparently ran in the family. "You're on. Let's go."

They disappeared, along with several more brothers,

in a flurry of shirttails and unbuckling belts into a back bedroom just as Melissa came from the kitchen, wiping her hands on a dish towel.

"I'm so glad you came." Joe's sister frowned as she gazed around the little entryway, then into the living room. "Where's Joe?"

Sara cocked her head in the direction the brothers had gone. "There," she said. "He's comparing scars with Mike and Danny and, um, I think it was Matt."

"I'm sure it was Matt." Melissa laughed. "He usually wins, too, with his appendectomy scar. Nobody's topped that one yet."

"And let's hope nobody ever does," Sara said.

Joe's sister hugged her hard and whispered, "Amen to that."

The Deckers' dining room table was nearly as big as the dining room. In fact, it was two tables pushed together in order to accommodate Rose and Mike and their nine children, plus spouses and significant others. There were twenty around the table. Sara counted seven pairs of eyes the exact same shade as Joe's and nine to-die-for grins.

No. Make that ten. Joe's father was using one just then at the head of the table where he was carving the first turkey.

Sara couldn't even remember the last time she and her parents had shared a holiday meal like this. They tended to travel over holidays. Last year on Thanksgiving Sara had ordered cashew chicken from King Ching, figuring it was as close to turkey as she was going to get.

She was wedged in beside Joe at a table groaning under two turkeys, a ham, mashed potatoes, three kinds of sweet potatoes, a pitcher of gravy and more vegetables than she had ever seen in a single meal. Just the passing of bowls turned into a happy challenge.

Joe reached for her hand under the table and whispered, "How're you doing, Campbell? We don't have to stay too long if you're—"

"Hush. I'm fine. This is the best Thanksgiving I've ever had."

"Me, too."

Then came the pies. Pumpkin, mincemeat, cinnamon apple and a lemon meringue that Rose had baked especially for Joe. When he finished the huge slice, he gave a little moan and leaned back in his chair. "I sure hope I don't get busted to patrolman, because I'd never fit in my uniform after this."

The whole table fell oddly silent for a moment, and Sara knew it was because they had come so close to losing him only a few weeks ago. Joe's father cleared his throat as if a painful little lump had lodged in it.

"So, when do you think you'll be going back to work, son?"

"Right after New Year's, Dad. I've got one more week of medical leave and then—" he slid his arm around Sara's shoulders "—I thought I'd take a little more vacation time so Sara and I could have a honeymoon."

She nearly choked on her last bite of pumpkin pie. They had talked about marriage and kids and a big old Victorian house, but those had been just dreamy discussions. Nothing official. No down-on-the-knees, ring-in-a-velvet-box proposal.

"A honeymoon! Oh, that's wonderful!" The words went around the table along with smiles and lifted wineglasses and thumbs-up.

"I thought we could fly down to a quiet little island in the Caribbean," he said, looking into her eyes. "What do you think, babe? Or fly to Hawaii."

Not only Joe's gray eyes were on her, but eighteen others, as well. "Is...is this a proposal?" she asked.

"It appears to be one." He did that grin. "What do you say? Want to take the Concorde to Paris or fly to Rio?"

"Oh, Joe." Sara started to laugh. The giggle worked its way up from her stomach, filled the back of her throat, then exploded in a burst of laughter she was helpless to control. The more bewildered Joe looked, the more she giggled—well, guffawed, actually—until tears started streaming down her face.

"Sara."

There was a hint of irritation in Joe's voice, and rightly so. He'd just proposed marriage in front of a score of witnesses, and the woman he'd asked to be his wife had promptly dissolved in gales of laughter, nearly flopping out of her chair.

"I'm sorry." Sara sat up straighter, swiped at her eyes and tried to pull herself together. "It's just that..." Another giggle got loose. "It's just that... I never told you. I'm afraid of flying, Joe."

Then it was the two of them laughing until their sides ached, until Sara was worried that Joe's stitches might come undone. The entire Decker clan was staring at them, stupefied, unable to understand what could possibly be so funny about a proposal of marriage or somebody's fear of flying.

"Okay," Joe said finally, barely managing to stifle his laughter. "How about a train to New York?"

"That would work," Sara said as she dabbed at her eyes with a corner of her napkin.

Across the table, Joe's brother Mike leaned forward. "I'm confused here. Are you two getting married, or what?"

Joe took her hand and kissed it, then whispered, "One thing at a time, Campbell. One thing at a time. First just say yes."

"Yes."

\* \* \* \* \*

*If you enjoyed*
**JUST ONE LOOK**
*be sure to watch for*
*Mary McBride's next book*
**BANDERA'S BRIDE**
*Coming in the spring of 2000*
*from Harlequin Historicals*

If you enjoyed what you just read,
then we've got an offer you can't resist!

# Take 2 bestselling love stories FREE!
# Plus get a FREE surprise gift!

**Clip this page and mail it to Silhouette Reader Service™**

**IN U.S.A.**
3010 Walden Ave.
P.O. Box 1867
Buffalo, N.Y. 14240-1867

**IN CANADA**
P.O. Box 609
Fort Erie, Ontario
L2A 5X3

**YES!** Please send me 2 free Silhouette Intimate Moments® novels and my free surprise gift. Then send me 6 brand-new novels every month, which I will receive months before they're available in stores. In the U.S.A., bill me at the bargain price of $3.57 plus 25¢ delivery per book and applicable sales tax, if any*. In Canada, bill me at the bargain price of $3.96 plus 25¢ delivery per book and applicable taxes**. That's the complete price and a savings of over 10% off the cover prices—what a great deal! I understand that accepting the 2 free books and gift places me under no obligation ever to buy any books. I can always return a shipment and cancel at any time. Even if I never buy another book from Silhouette, the 2 free books and gift are mine to keep forever. So why not take us up on our invitation. You'll be glad you did!

245 SEN CNFF
345 SEN CNFG

| | |
|---|---|
| Name | (PLEASE PRINT) |
| Address | Apt.# |
| City | State/Prov. | Zip/Postal Code |

\* Terms and prices subject to change without notice. Sales tax applicable in N.Y.
\*\* Canadian residents will be charged applicable provincial taxes and GST.
  All orders subject to approval. Offer limited to one per household.
  ® are registered trademarks of Harlequin Enterprises Limited.

# Don't miss Silhouette's newest cross-line promotion,

*Four royal sisters find their own Prince Charmings as they embark on separate journeys to find their missing brother, the Crown Prince!*

The search begins in October 1999 and continues through February 2000:

On sale October 1999: **A ROYAL BABY ON THE WAY**
by award-winning author **Susan Mallery** (Special Edition)

On sale November 1999: **UNDERCOVER PRINCESS**
by bestselling author **Suzanne Brockmann** (Intimate Moments)

On sale December 1999: **THE PRINCESS'S WHITE KNIGHT**
by popular author **Carla Cassidy** (Romance)

On sale January 2000: **THE PREGNANT PRINCESS**
by rising star **Anne Marie Winston** (Desire)

On sale February 2000: **MAN…MERCENARY…MONARCH**
by top-notch talent **Joan Elliott Pickart** (Special Edition)

## ROYALLY WED
Only in—
## SILHOUETTE BOOKS

Available at your favorite retail outlet.

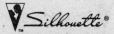

Visit us at www.romance.net

SSERW

**INTIMATE MOMENTS®**

*Silhouette®*

invites you to join the Brand brothers,
a close-knit Texas family in which each sibling
is eventually branded by love—and marriage!

# MAGGIE SHAYNE

**continues her intriguing series**

**with**

## THE OUTLAW BRIDE, IM #967

On sale December 1999

*If you missed the first five tales of
the irresistible Brand brothers:*

**THE LITTLEST COWBOY**, IM #716 $3.99 U.S./$4.50 CAN.
**THE BADDEST VIRGIN IN TEXAS**, IM #788 $3.99 U.S./$4.50 CAN.
**BADLANDS BAD BOY**, IM #809 $3.99 U.S./$4.50 CAN.
**THE HUSBAND SHE COULDN'T REMEMBER**, IM #854 $4.25 U.S./$4.75 CAN.
**THE BADDEST BRIDE IN TEXAS**, IM #907 $4.25 U.S./$4.75 CAN.

*you can order them now.*